NULLO

DONALD DEWEY

MILFORD HOUSE
an imprint of Sunbury Press, Inc.
Mechanicsburg, PA USA

MILFORD HOUSE

an imprint of Sunbury Press, Inc.
Mechanicsburg, PA USA

FIRST MILFORD HOUSE PRESS EDITION: April 2021

Set in Adobe Garamond | Interior design by Crystal Devine | Cover design by Lawrence Knorr | Edited by Lawrence Knorr.

Publisher's Cataloging-in-Publication Data
Names: Dewey, Donald, author.
Title: Nullo / Donald Dewey.
Description: First trade paperback edition. | Mechanicsburg, PA : Milford House Press, 2021.
Summary: A reporter for a New York daily, Danny receives a deus ex machina for his frazzled life when a bureaucratic snafu sends the wrong coffin from Italy. Soon, he finds himself assigned to Rome to escort the sister of the man who should have been in the coffin. As he accompanies her dance through Italian red tape, he realizes two things -- that he is in love with her and that he is far more interested in the story of the Italian whose body had been sent to New York than in that of her deceased brother. The dilemma becomes only more complicated when a third body is found to have been misplaced and when one of the three turns out not to be very dead.
Identifiers: ISBN : 978-1-62006-503-7 (softcover).
Subjects: FICTION / Mystery & Detective / International Crime & Mystery | FICTION / Mystery & Detective / Amateur Sleuth | FICTION / Romance / Suspense.

Product of the United States of America
0 1 1 2 3 5 8 13 21 34 55

Continue the Enlightenment!

For Monique Henon and Nello Ciolli

| 1 |

ALTHOUGH I DIDN'T know it then, Nullo Borgato was flying into my life while I was running down a block full of pedestrians. In the strict traffic sense, they weren't pedestrians at all, but Jackson Heights Latinos sitting on their stoops and idling in front of their stores, passing a sunny fall Sunday afternoon by jawing with one another or listening to their radios. They assumed sidewalks were for walkers and talkers, with the streets for cars. Joe McAteer didn't share their assumption.

Joe was my father-in-law. I like saying that. It has the ring of a fact false for being true. What I was slower to appreciate that Sunday after-noon was Joe's solution for the creeping Roosevelt Avenue traffic that was making him late for his weekly dinner at the Hofbrau. Behind some muttering that the spics had caused the snarl by not staying below the Panama Canal, he had simply nosed his 25-year-old Ford out of the traf-fic lane, grazed a stanchion of the elevated train, and trundled up onto the sidewalk. Since it took me long seconds even to become speechless, Annie let out the first shout from the front seat. Joe's response was to hit the gas pedal harder and start the meter in his eyes on the number of Hispanics he was scattering into doorways and between parked cars. With only his reflection in the rearview mirror to judge by, I wasn't sure of his demonic count, but he seemed to like it.

The scurrying people aside, my most immediate thought was that there was nothing—no fruit stands, no gaping cellar door, no pavement work—likely to cause *us* harm. Even as I was bouncing up and down in the back and cautioning myself to leave the shrieking to Annie, I was clinging to some unearned presumption that we would make the intersection at the far curb without smashing or falling into something. Call it an innate optimism—or just my determination not to be impressed by the latest Joe McAteer gesture. Granted, he had never risked vehicular homicide before, but after almost five years of living with his daughter, I had foreseen *something* coming after Annie had told him we were going to get a divorce. How could I not have expected it? This was the guy who had once asked a cousin in the FBI to check me out as a prospective son-in-law, who had come to our Manhattan apartment for a Christmas dinner only on the condition that he could bring along a priest-friend for exorcising the evil spirits from our living room, and who had taken to calling my editor to denounce me as a slimy liberal if one of my articles implied there was more to life than cracking down on welfare cheats. In a way, the Flying Latinos of Roosevelt Avenue were an inevitable act in the Joe McAteer Circus.

And he got away with it. There was screaming in English and Spanish, then the clank of something heavy and metallic on the trunk, but he reached the next street safely, bounced back down off the sidewalk, and veered off right, away from all the witnesses on the avenue. It took me a couple of blocks to accept that no patrol cars were coming after us and another couple to get over my resentment at the NYPD's priorities. By that time Annie had controlled her own shaking in the front seat and was launched into as direct assault on her father as I had ever heard. "But you could've killed those people! Suppose one of them had fallen trying to get away? . . . Daddy?"

Daddy didn't bother answering. As Annie and I should have understood, apparently, the day's theme wasn't running down people on sidewalks, but ending marriages that should have never taken place to begin with. Hadn't he warned her five years ago? Hadn't he especially warned her about getting involved with a dago?

I waited for Annie to look around at me in exasperation. I'm still waiting. It was another small announcement we were kaput: Even if she needed an ally against her father's dementia, it wasn't going to be me. She had learned to distrust temporary alliances.

So why was I even in the car to begin with? Mainly because I had gotten tired of slinking away for Daddy Joe. Ever since Annie and I had decided to split up, he had been all crust with her, and I hadn't looked forward to another Sunday evening of seeing her trudge back from visiting him with the beaten expression of somebody who had been through another trial for both of us. Maybe with me along, I had thought, he would keep some of his poison to himself; maybe, at the very least, he would confine his purple-faced rages to all the Thems who were destroying America. If Annie had resisted the idea, I would have been content to stay buried all afternoon on the couch under the *Times*. But not only had she just nodded at my suggestion, she hadn't even bothered tipping him off I was coming along—a detail I hadn't learned until we had gotten off the train and had been within sight of his house. That's when more of my optimism had sprung forth. What I had wanted to think was that she was anticipating his dismay in opening the door. "Yeah, take a look, Daddy," I had fancied her saying at the moment of truth. "Okay, he's the lousy husband you said he was, but he's not that yellow guinea you're always going on about. Say hello."

So much for fantasies. What I had forgotten was that McAteer was the kind who dressed up two hours before an appointment and then stood in his topcoat at a window watching for his visitors. By the time he had opened the front door of his neat brick house, he had had all the time necessary for dulling the disdain in his eyes, composing his granite jaw, and memorizing the colorless information that "the car's over there." As he had backed down into us to get at the lock with his key, even the *Times* Real Estate section had looked good to me.

All by way of saying that only a few hours before getting entangled with Nullo Borgato, Joe McAteer had represented all the spics and guineas in *my* world. Why bother examining the reasons for my split with Annie as long as that gargoyle was around? For me Daddy Joe was more than a scapegoat ethnic group, he was an entire scapegoat species—the spine-straight, white-haired 60-year-old Irish Catholic who regarded grunting and praying as the only legitimate forms of conversation.

And then there was Oscar.

McAteer's regular waiter at the Hofbrau, Oscar was a decaying misanthrope who negotiated the restaurant floor with his huge silver trays like someone who had been taught to walk by Boris Karloff and who would have been equally content serving his customers to boars and steers as the other way around. The man's line in visceral contempt was infinite. Not once in my half-dozen times at the restaurant had I heard him compliment anyone or admit even begrudging wonder before some world event. Everybody born was "a jerk vaiting to get vot he shood." The daily scandals and hypocrisies that comforted even the radio talk show morons were, for Oscar, only more proof that the planet had to be wiped clean, no exceptions made for giggling babies, kittens, or fawns. If the man had any saving grace, it was that he wasn't fascinating even in his mountainous bile. He was oppressive, not romantic. And if you were tempted to forget it, he made sure to intersperse his snortings about the world with whining about the most recent diner who had undertipped him or about the pustules on his feet that made it still more irritating for him to have to stand around waiting for people like us to make up our minds about what to order.

None of this fazed Joe McAteer, though. At some point over his years of patronizing the Hofbrau, he had anointed Oscar as a comic, and his first sight of the old slug scraping through the tables was enough to bring a feline sparkle to his eyes. Did Oscar even remember Joe McAteer's name between weekly credit card transactions? If I had my doubts, I was the only one who did. Joe looked perilously close to gratitude for being back in the company of someone who was his match—even his better—in sourness.

"How are you today, Oscar?"

"Today, tomorrow. Vat's da difference?"

If it had been anybody but me next to him, I think McAteer would have nudged me with his elbow; as it was, he was content to nod before so much drollery. Then, after Oscar had gone off with the drink order, he delivered a jab anyway. It was a four-word announcement, addressed to the front door. "I've redone my will."

When Annie was mystified, she tried to look peppy, as though urging one more hint to understand a riddle. "Redone it how?"

"What I'm not leaving to the Church, I'm leaving to your children."

I imagined the bubbles in my water magnifying until they were the ugly cesspools popping in my chest.

"Daddy, I told you . . ."

McAteer finally looked away from the door, to reach for his napkin and flap it over his lap. "Yeah, you told me. But I don't think you get over one whim by having another one. So maybe you both better think twice. I want to help you think twice."

"You can't do things like that, Daddy."

"Well, I did."

"But it's . . ."

"Cruel," I finally mustered.

He thought I was as comical as Oscar. "Oh, hear this now! And you're an expert in that, right? You're ditching her, but me looking out for my money, that's what's cruel."

I knew I showed too much helplessness looking at Annie. Neither of us had expected anything but awkward evasions for the afternoon. But first with the bumper ride on Roosevelt Avenue and now with the will, McAteer had clearly been preparing only for frontal charges.

"This isn't about money, Daddy. You want to give it all to the Church, give it to them. It's about being nasty."

"Change your minds and I might change mine."

"And that'd make you happy, Joe? We might be miserable, but as long as you get what you want, it'll be okay?"

"You wouldn't be so miserable if you'd live like normal people."

"Normal people."

He turned on me so quickly I knew he had put some rehearsing into saying: "You live in that dusty apartment not big enough for one. No wonder you're always on each other's nerves. And why're you there? Because you got two jobs and that makes you proud you can afford some place with a Manhattan address. What a normal person does is get his wife to quit her job, start a family, and move into a decent house."

It wasn't the first time McAteer's logic had sent me staggering down a greased hill, but I wasn't up for parsing his mind (or for admitting that the part about our apartment wasn't *that* loony). "Let me spell it out for you, Joe. It's not me you're hurting with this crap because I'll be out of the picture. It's Annie you're hurting."

I still cringe thinking about that little outburst. For all the arguments, tears, and leaden silences Annie and I had been inflicting on each other for more than a year, our split had never sounded as irrevocable as it did at that moment in the restaurant. Breaking up was exactly what it said—not some neat, single cut, but piece after piece falling away amid an ongoing shock that there were always more and bigger pieces to be dispatched. I needed every muscle I had to keep my eyes trained on McAteer's beet face and not have to see how Annie was reacting.

"Everybody gets hurt," he said. "The only thing that matters is what you do about it."

Oscar's arrival with the drinks gave me the courage to look at Annie again. I didn't understand why she couldn't hear me—begging her to stand throw her napkin on the table, make some appropriate fuck-you declaration, and march out. Was it just because I didn't actually *say* anything?

Then Oscar made everything moot. No sooner had he set down Annie's red wine, McAteer's Presbyterian, and my Bloody Mary than he took a lurching step backward and got all his phlegm into "You don't got dem?"

McAteer readied another smile. "What's that, Oscar?"

"Bread! Menus! Vot else?"

The fat couple at the next table heard the delirium as plainly as I did. But they couldn't see the glistening patch of perspiration on the old man's forehead or the popped eyes that didn't have a clue about what they were seeing. I was still reaching for the thought HEART ATTACK when Oscar grabbed at the black Bics in his shirt pocket, dropped his hand uselessly, then staggered back into the heavy woman, clipping her ear with the edge of his tray. She let out a yelp that seemed to pull me out of my chair as much as the reeling Oscar or the clattering tray. But even as I got my hands around the old man to steady him, the woman sounded abruptly back in control, letting go with a "Frank!" that was all command for her husband to close his mouth, put down his fork, and do something useful.

"No, no, no!"

I didn't ask no what. Maybe Oscar was railing against the gods for choosing that specific moment for whisking him off to Valhalla or maybe he just didn't want me going through his pockets for the heart pills I wanted to believe were in one of them. Either way, I had enough trouble fending off the surprising strength of his mottled hand while yelling for some doctor in the house to get up from his *schnitzel* and help. "Heart pills, Oscar! Do you have any heart pills?"

"Get it over vit!"

The fat man named Frank finally got to his feet to open a seating possibility for Oscar. There was no more color in the waiter's face, and the forehead sweat that had been only a patch had spread over his knobby bald head. His breathing came louder, more rapidly, and his eyes seemed to roll in terror that Frank and I were trying to suffocate what remained of it by insisting on lowering him into Frank's chair. "Get it over vit!" he demanded again—not just as in "Leave me alone!" or "Let me die in peace!" but with the scorn of "Let me stop having to see your stupid faces!"

And then, thank Christ, he closed his blind, angry eyes and conked out.

The next few minutes passed like a pantomime by the Helpless and the Concerned. The manager appeared with a glass of water and a frown at how his customers had been put out by so much commotion. The bartender yelled over that he had gotten through to the EMS. A busboy stood hobbled in an aisle holding a pitcher of water as though waiting for an order to dump it on the floor. Some of the diners braved getting up from their places for a closer look. Frank, now fully in charge, kept a thumb on Oscar's pulse, monitoring every beat between anxious looks over to the door for the arrival of the paramedics, while Mrs. Frank kept rubbing his back as though her husband was the one with the problem. As for Oscar himself, he just kept pumping his chest under his starched white shirt, plumbing deeper and deeper for power with every exhale. A glob of spit in the corner of his mouth seemed already to have gelled from neglect.

I sat back down at my table. Most of the diners looked afraid of going back to eat, worried it would be considered indelicate, but I saw no reason not to swig my Bloody Mary. Annie seemed to be expecting something more from me, but she had for a long time. On the other hand, she hadn't turned around back in the car for my solidarity against her father, so I returned the favor by taking a second swig.

McAteer kept his eyes on the table, compulsively grinding his index finger into the tablecloth. I envied how neatly his nail had been manicured. I also would have liked to have driven a spike through the hard grating sound he was making. Then the paramedics came bustling in with their black bags and gurney, and he allowed himself to raise his eyes from his finger to the circle Frank, the manager, and two waiters had made around Oscar. The older blond of the EMS team needed all of 15 seconds to examine Oscar and pronounce the sigh of sighs. McAteer heard the verdict, but his craggy face didn't change. I hadn't expected it to. There was nothing new to expect from Joe McAteer, marriages, wills, or the stone cruelties that went into all those things. The old shit sitting dead a few feet away had said it for me too, I thought: Just get it over with.

| 2 |

FOUR HOURS LATER, I was safely back at the paper listening to Ed Minton going on about Nullo Borgato. Whenever the managing editor invited me to sit down at his desk, I knew I was about to hear something he viewed as a major feature. Part of the ritual was I was supposed to understand that without showing I did.

"HST called from Kennedy," he said, trying to look casual about the cigarette he was holding under his desk, out of sight of any passing anti-smoke Nazis in the office. "They have a body out there from Italy. The sister of the deceased and her undertaker showed up last night, but it's not the brother she was expecting. Instead, we got a . . ." He made using his free hand to pick up his pad look like a juggling feat. "Nullo Borgato."

"No neighborhood."

"What?"

"Nullo Borgato. You can translate it as no neighborhood."

Minton found me irritating enough to lean down for another puff. He was a short, bony man only a couple of years away from retirement and not in the least melancholy about the prospect. Little that had happened around the paper in the last 20 years—the ban against smoking, the installation of computers, the executive decision to turn the third page over to celebrity gossip—had been to his liking. Any last shot at sentimentality over his three decades in the building had evaporated when his most recent assistant, a TV-trained hotshot named Frolich, had been promoted above him. Now, as he liked to remind me and anybody else, he ran into at The Ink downstairs, he was just hanging on so "they don't screw me out of my pension, too."

"That's really great to know," he said, coming back up to me. "But whatever the hell his name means, he's not John Iler and that's who Barbara Iler's interested in. HST says she's really in a mood about this. Calls to the State Department, Italian Embassy, the whole nine yards."

I pictured some old sister of Oscar's waiting for his body in Vienna or Frankfurt and discovering she had been shipped Joe McAteer instead. "If it was my brother, I guess I'd get excited, too."

Minton glared as though I had strummed one of his patience strings too hard. "You following me here or not?"

"Yeah. Barbara Iler's fuming because they sent her the wrong body."

"And?"

"And you want me to go talk to her and get all the usual. . . ." I shut up. I had been invited to sit down, I reminded myself; the standard interview with the Iler woman about the torments of bureaucracies wouldn't have merited more than a summons to Minton's office and a curt order to follow up on what he had scribbled down on his pad.

"Good," he said. "Silence is golden. Now, in your profound eagerness to think instead of just jerk your knee, tell me how many stories I'm talking about here. Don't rush it, Danny. Take all the time you need. An hour. A day. Two years till I retire."

I didn't dare believe my first thought. "Borgato?"

He dipped down for another puff; down where his recently liberal Travel and Expenses policy was. "We got a doubleheader here," he said, after rejoining me again. "We got the Iler woman finding out her brother's not coming to the funeral she's invited everybody to. Plus . . ."

"Iler's still over there!" I said, admitting the delicious. "Who screwed up? Who signed off on the foul-up? Is Iler in Borgato's grave? How do they dig him up without making a big scene out of it and adding to the grief of the Borgato family?"

"That's good, Danny. Sometimes—not often, but every once in a while—you repay my faith in you."

I realize now it was all more logical than it had first sounded in Minton's office; a trip to Italy *should* have been in the cards for me. The story was a natural for a managing editor whose notion of human interest didn't start and end with the name of the sperm bank fathering the latest child of a 50-year-old Hollywood actress. Fred Cleary, the paper's Rome stringer, was a lush who had been left behind from the days of *La Dolce Vita*. Minton had been embarked for months on a spending campaign ultimately aimed at getting him into some brawl of principle with Frolich over who worried about the news and who fretted only about the corporate bottom line. And lastly, I had never minded annoying people with my "no neighborhood" revelations, to show them I hadn't wasted my three years of Italian at NYU and my childhood memories of Italian family dinners.

But all that logic came later. However, many the reasons that made Nullo Borgato's flying corpse a good story and me the obvious reporter to cover it, I have to admit my first reaction was nothing more than GETTING AWAY. It was such a nakedly unprofessional response I figured that was why Minton gave me one of his longest scowls, then dropped down under the desk again.

| 3 |

I HAD TO wait until Monday afternoon to talk to HST. Our Kennedy Airport informant had earned his nickname inevitably enough: His real name was Harry Turman. Harry Turman—not Truman—worked for airport administration and had been dropping the odd quarter on Minton for about five years, ever since he had picked up a few bucks for inside information on a near-miss between two United flights over Queens. Talking to Turman was no treat. He was more paranoid than a political defector, and I had to go through a rigmarole of calling him at his office, telling him I had the tickets for the Mets (or Knicks or Rangers) game, then hanging up to wait for him to get back to me on Minton's line. When he called back, he had to be reassured constantly that nobody but Minton and the reporter he was speaking with knew of his existence. It wouldn't have done much for his fidgets to know that even Minton played "HST" downstairs at The Ink. This was a game where all those gathered under the dewy-fingered influence of martinis tried to find a better reverse anagram for him than the obvious Harry S. Truman, such as He's So Tense or Harry's So Talkative. Okay, it wasn't "Jeopardy," but the person voted the best variation got a free round on the losers.

Anyway, after we had gone through all the usual security procedures, Turman showed again why he had his valuable moments by giving me Barbara Iler's address and phone number on the Upper East Side. The place turned out to be a freshly scraped four-floor walk-up on 84th Street between First and Second avenues. Annie and I had lived only two blocks away on a six-month sublet immediately after getting married, and the neighborhood seemed like its pleasantly smelly self, only a little more so. Add one more Hungarian deli, one more dark restaurant where you brought along your own wine, and one more black garbage bag on the sidewalk the Sanitation Department took its time about collecting. I liked being back but didn't like feeling a century removed from the small additions.

What had I expected from Barbara Iler? Minton's world-weariness and HST's minced particulars had both suggested a tallish, resolute woman, probably wearing a sensibly tailored black suit in honor of her dead brother, maybe accustomed to mentioning the existence of a family lawyer when she didn't like the turn of the conversation. I hadn't quite gotten that in calling her for an appointment, but I had called her on my cellphone—always a nubless pencil for sketching people. Climbing the stairs to her top-floor apartment, I was still preparing myself for somebody on either side of 50 on bereavement leave from a high managerial position with a bank or insurance company. And how was any of *that* going to make the chatting easier on the flight to Italy that, according to HST, she had booked for the following evening? Not only wasn't she expecting a traveling companion, she was probably going to resist having one.

At least I was right about the tall part. Barbara Iler, a lanky 5'8" or 5'9", stood at the top of the stairs in her stockinged feet, gray slacks, and gray turtleneck. Her smile was more curiosity than suspicion, and she shook my hand with a crack about all the friends she had lost because of her stairs. She said it in such a laconic, throaty whisper I wondered if HST had cut some corners by directing me to the first Barbara Iler he had found in the phone book.

The living room she led me into was the cramped front of a railroad flat overflowing with books on the floor and bright prints and posters of animals on the walls. Aside from a computer work nook near the room's single window, the furniture was second-hand stuff that came from garage sales or Park Avenue sidewalks before Sanitation's weekly pickups. None of it said Aetna office supervisor.

"This is all so ridiculous, isn't it?" she smiled nervously when we were both seated. "I can't believe it's gotten so fouled up."

I assured her strange things were always happening under the heavens, then went on to say a few dozen other tinny things. Even tinnier were my thoughts. While she walked me through some of the details of how her brother John ("Johnny") had succumbed to a heart attack, how he had ended up in Rome to do it, and how she had been dismayed to read the wrong nameplate on the casket in a Kennedy service hangar, I kept poking away at all my wrong expectations. She wasn't 50, but about 35, with a small, tight doe face and a black crewcut with an upstroke in front. She was the startled one in the college yearbook—elegance and innocence somehow working against one another and leaving her to wonder what the world had in store for her. If she had been severe with the people at the airport, going the "whole nine yards," as Minton had put it, it had probably taken more out of her than them. Lacing and unlacing her long, ringless fingers as she leaned forward from her settee, she could barely get her soft voice to criticize the screwups even in the third person. All the Italian and American bureaucrats were just part of something "crazy."

And then my tinniest thought of all: She was talking about her brother, wasn't she? Where was her grief, her outrage? They must have played and fought together as kids, shared secrets behind the backs of their parents. Where were the red rims of her eyes about that? Why did she have to keep talking about "Johnny" as just one more detail of a baffling international idiocy?

"And that's about as much as I know," she said, deliberately stilling her fingers. "I suppose it's funny in a way."

"Would your brother have thought so?"

She looked at me as though I had just walked in, thought about the question a second, then smiled. "Yes, I think so. Johnny liked chaos. He said order was only an accident."

My first thought was that she was matching me tinniness for tinniness: that Johnny Iler had never said anything of the kind in his life and she just wanted to bring him back to life for me if not for her. Then she wrapped her wrists around her knee and rocked back and forth a couple of times. It took me a second to see she was fighting back the tears I had decided were missing from her genes.

"Johnny knew his heart could go at any time," she finally went on. "The doctors really shouldn't have told him. It was his last excuse for cutting off people, all he needed to crawl up in his cave and close the rock in front of it. The cave happened to be Italy."

"What was he doing over there, anyway?"

"For a living? Teaching English in some school. But that was just to keep his body and soul together. He was doing some kind of research. He was always very secretive about it."

"About language?"

I heard my tone, too: *He was looking for a new letter in the alphabet?* She forgave me. "I have no idea. He was very good at being secretive."

I closed off my broken dam of fantasy—proof that extraterrestrials were living in Ethiopia? evidence that Jesus Christ and Attila the Hun had been the same person?—before she could see it. But even with my mouth shut I couldn't keep quiet. One second, I was reminding myself that John Iler's mysterious research wasn't the story, that I was only concerned with his missing body, and the next second she was giving the slightest defensive toss to her chin as she stared over at me through the glare of the sun coming through the window. "Not what you're interested in?"

"Of course, it is."

"You haven't written anything."

My notebook on my knee suddenly felt like an encyclopedia. "I didn't want to interrupt you."

Everything could have ended right then and there. Even as a tactful lie, it smelled rancid. I thanked the Kleenex. Instead of getting up and going into another room for something to dry her eyes, earning herself a few seconds away for making a clear-headed decision to get rid of me, she spotted a tissue in the corner of the settee and used that for dabbing. "I can hardly expect people who never met Johnny to feel strongly about him," she said. "I'm his sister and there were lots of times not even I felt close to him. He could be very icy, and I seemed to annoy him a lot."

"You make him sound like an ogre."

She was delighted with me for some bad reason. "The ogres are over there," she said, pointing to her computer. "I write stories for kids."

What was the old comedy routine? I WRITE STORIES FOR CHILDREN. CHILDREN LIKE MY STORIES. I LIKE CHILDREN TO LIKE MY STORIES. DO YOU LIKE MY STORIES? DO YOU LIKE STORIES FOR CHILDREN? Something like that. And that was about as appropriate as I could be as her gaze lingered over the work nook, making her look genuinely uncertain whether she would have preferred her brother to have been an ogre.

"Then he wouldn't have baffled you so much?"

She nodded without hesitation. "I make up ogres and monsters and witches," she said in another whisper. "And what you make up you don't have to believe in, right?"

"Right," I said, no idea what either of us was talking about.

| 4 |

MINTON WASN'T IMPRESSED I had muddled through my entrance exam with Barbara Iler. His reaction was just a gruntier version of her shrug when I had told her the paper's intentions: She didn't own Alitalia and couldn't stop me from booking a seat on her flight even if she had wanted to. What I didn't tell him was that I was the one who had left the East Side walk-up with a doubt or two about the necessity of crossing the Atlantic.

I told Annie, instead—over some tenth "Masterpiece Theater" rerun of British squires greeting each other with waves of their walking sticks and tips of their Dr. Seuss hats. But since I wasn't feeling *that* shabby about intruding upon Barbara Iler in her grief, since Barbara Iler wasn't *that* hostile to my company, and since the assignment wasn't *quite* as much about the two dead people as about the invisible forces that had plastered the wrong release forms on the wrong caskets, Annie didn't *quite* understand what was bothering me. And then to ensure that the travails of the Iler and Borgato families wouldn't even make the Top Ten of concerns for the evening before I took off for Rome, I said: "I'm not sure I should be involved in this at all. I know it's my job, but I feel like a fifth wheel, some actor who's been hired for a play that has no part for him."

"Welcome to the club."

It went downhill from there. Even the square buckles on the hats of the PBS squires were more fascinating than the dialogue from our couch. And by now Annie was able to deliver it in a monotone that seemed wasteful of her naturally puffy mouth. I no longer thought of her as remote because that implied some obscure place I would never reach or recognize even if I did. On the contrary, I knew exactly where she had gone—deep inside her billowy peasant blouse and chunky shoulders, deep inside her gray eyes and Chiclet-neat teeth and smells of onions and Camay. The problem was, she wasn't remote in the least, she was as close as she had ever been. *That* was the distance that had grown between us.

How had it gotten that far? The fact was, I didn't trust any answer I came up with. If it came from me, it had to be glib, evasive, artificial. If it came from her, it had to be accusatory, expedient, artificial. The best I managed had been one evening with Minton at The Ink, when I had still distrusted every word out of my mouth but had slipped too fast into a couple of martinis not to suspect a need to say *some*thing to *some*body. Annie and I got along thinking about today, tomorrow, and next week, I had told him. But whenever we lifted our heads to look further, we both got a little dizzy. So it became easier not to talk about getting a bigger apartment or about where we wanted to be with our jobs a couple of years down the road. It became especially easier not to talk about having kids. In fact, to seal up that conversation for good, we had gotten into the habit of not even going near one another around that time of the month. And from there it had been little trouble at all to stay away from each other for the whole month, then the month after it and the month after that one, too. If we didn't go to a party every once in a while and drink a lot of eggnog around Christmas, we could have made the entire year chaste! What did he think that added up to?

Minton hadn't asked for that kind of a confidence; he had looked uncomfortable with every word, only some kind of office obligation to one of his employees seeming to stop him from shutting me up. He had all but sighed with relief in pushing our empty glasses toward Sal the bartender. "I've never been good at arithmetic," he had shrugged. "Even the kindergarten kind." And of course, he had been right. There *had* been nothing else to say. One and one was always two.

The theme of themes in front of "Masterpiece Theater" was the whens and hows of making good on the announcement we had already made to her father, not to mention ourselves. And Joe McAteer wasn't the only one to be considered. There was Oscar, whose collapse in front of our eyes should have been good for spurring us into a final move. There was Connie, Annie's fellow accountant at work who had apparently memorized every statistic ever compiled about marriage, divorce, and fertility years. There was even the landlord, who had just mailed another lease for signing and who couldn't be expected to shoulder the burden of having both of us walk out in separate directions after only a few months.

"Like I really give a damn about that."

"No, you only worry about being insensitive to this widow."

"His sister, not his widow."

"A plan, Danny! I need a plan!"

"Then make one. You don't have to wait for me."

"Okay, then. And if you come back from Italy and find all your stuff packed up, that's all right?"

"I'm only going for a few days."

"That's enough time."

A little-known fact about epiphanies is that they have as many stages as the rockets launched by NASA. For example, I had been startled into resolve at the Hofbrau to move away from all the McAteers once and for all. But until Annie looked at me so starkly that night on the couch, a professional accountant reporting merely what her audit of the revenues and expenses had told her, I had been waiting even for my epiphanies to proceed through their successive phases from propulsion to *real* propulsion to *really real* propulsion. Except Annie wasn't buying: We were on our way into the cosmos or we weren't.

"You'd really do that?"

"No victims or aggressors at this point, okay?"

She didn't expect the scullery maid on the TV screen to argue with her, so I didn't, either. An hour later I had made a good start on the things she would box for me while I was away. At least for the mound of clothes and tschotschkes I had piled into a corner under the bedroom window, I could have just been preparing for where Ed Minton wanted to send me.

| 5 |

IT WASN'T UNTIL I got to Kennedy that I realized how serious Minton was about having an executive suite showdown with Frolich over his spending ways: The ticket I had shoved into my shoulder-bag in the office without looking turned out to be first-class. As I giddily made my way to the waiting area, I could hear Minton arguing that the Italians were sure to have booked Barbara Iler first-class and that part of my job was to talk with her on the flight to Rome. Less giddily, I could also hear Frolich rebutting that I should have already picked up enough from her in New York and, besides, wasn't the thrust of the story locating John Iler's body and talking to the Italians who had misplaced it? I didn't like making Frolich's case even mentally and decided that was something else I could blame on Annie: Share a hamper with a bean counter, start thinking like one.

Barbara Iler was standing near the boarding gate with a middle-aged couple. She looked taller than she had in her apartment—plausible enough since she was now wearing shoes. But my impression was also helped by the squat builds of the couple, the long black dress she did own after all, and the tiny black leather bag that hung on a spaghetti strap from her shoulder to her hip. I barely had time for the misgiving that she was traveling with friends or relatives when she glanced over at me, gave the slightest shake of her head, then leaned back down to whatever the woman at her shoulder was saying. Some things got through even to me.

I subsided into a seat, adding up her stiff politeness and the couple's lack of hand luggage as official people who were there to make sure the Italian government was more scrupulous about dispatching live bodies than it had been dead ones.

The Italians remained near the boarding gate after Barbara went off with handshakes. They kept their eyes so glued to her as she headed into the plane that I had to go around them. My years at NYU and around my grandmother's table had been good for understanding the man's mutter of *speriamo che*, but I was out of earshot before I could hear exactly what it was he was hoping.

"I didn't think it would make anyone's job easier if they knew what you were doing," Barbara said inside. "I have their names if you want to talk to them when you come back."

I didn't know which part of her tact flustered me more: the part about handling the Embassy pair or the part about taking one of the big white seats on the aisle so I could take the opposite aisle seat—close enough for talking, but not so close we were mistaken for traveling companions. I was beginning to feel intimidated by the ease with which others seemed to do the correct thing.

It took a couple of Bloody Marys, a veal piccata, and the dimming of the cabin lights for the in-flight movie for me to get across the aisle— and then mainly because a guy behind me made it obvious he preferred watching Denzel Washington to hearing about John Iler. Even without a headset for the movie, I could see his point. The way his sister told it, when Iler hadn't been acting secretive about whatever it was that fascinated him, he had been a hypochondriac who had felt vindicated by the discovery that, at 37, he had the heart of somebody 30 years older.

"But that kind of condition must've been building for years. Why did it take so long to find it?"

"Johnny was a hypochondriac, but he hated doctors. If he hadn't fainted on a street one night and been taken to Emergency, they might never have known. He diagnosed all his own ailments and was very proud of himself when one of them turned out actually to exist."

"Great pastime."

"I suppose it had its advantages."

"Like what?"

She brightened so quickly I sensed she was picking and choosing—what might be told to a reporter, what might be told to a disinterested stranger, what she wanted to keep for herself. "Like parties. He'd go to a party, look around, see if there was somebody to his liking, then get a drink, go over to a corner, and start radiating misery. It always worked."

"What did?"

"There'd always be some woman who'd gravitate toward him to ask him what was wrong. And Johnny would say 'I'm sick' or 'I'm dying' or something melodramatic like that, and before you knew it, all her maternal instincts were going."

"He must've had something going for him besides that spiel."

"It wasn't a spiel. He really did believe he was sick or dying."

"But I mean underneath that he must've been a good-looking guy or told funny stories or something."

She gave me the same defensive cock of the chin she had in her apartment. "Is there anything more appealing than believing what you say? I imagine some people can be drawn to other things, but I never have." She ran both palms over her knees, then let out a nervous laugh. "And that's what I just had Wise Owlie tell all the other birds in the forest!"

I laughed more than I had to. Wise Owlie seemed like a safer thought than how John Iler had bedded down women with his misery gambit, how Barbara Iler definitely had something of the spooky about her, and how I felt like running my own palms over her knees.

| 6 |

THE WELCOMING COMMITTEE at Fiumicino Airport was a beanpole from the American Embassy named Chester Winans. His instructions had been to pick up Barbara and drive her to the Via Veneto, where more senior types would take over with the apologies and promises. What his instructions hadn't prepared him for was Barbara introducing me as the second member of her party. "Chet," as he wanted us to call him, first tried the high road of seeing me as a family member who only incidentally worked for a newspaper. Disabused of that notion as we waited for our bags, he excused himself to make a call. More than five minutes later he came back with the air of being charged with a heavier assignment. "I'm afraid arrangements have been made only for one," he said, keeping his eyes midway between us. "There was no advisory about the media . . ."

"All I really need is a lift into the city. Can you manage that?"

He could. And on the drive in I could identify with his awkwardness at the baggage claim. I had a little more on my hands than I had counted on, too. Chet was so relieved not to be bearing trouble to his embassy superiors that he couldn't gush enough about his childhood visits to New York from Wilkes-Barre. He was my friend, my ingratiating chauffeur, my fellow American on the oddly foreign European landscape, and I didn't want to listen to any of them. I wasn't overwhelmed, either, by the colorless assortment of cement works, hilltop apartment complexes, and scraggy chicken coops that flew by my window between endless billboards for cordials and movies. What had been that thought back in Minton's office about getting away? Considering the fact that I was only a few minutes into my first trip to Europe, there was far too much of the familiar, the banal, or both around me.

And then there was the real source of my uneasiness sitting silently behind me.

Barbara hadn't opened her mouth since getting into the car. Okay, Chet Winans wasn't the one to provide her with the latest news on what had been done to locate her brother's body. But in her place, wouldn't I have at least asked enough to have him tell me that? Wouldn't I have projected enough sorrow to slow down his happy-headed monologue about Circle Line cruises and East Village clubs? I didn't blame him for that, I blamed her.

The late morning traffic inside Rome restored some order. Chet forgot about Wilkes-Barre Meets Christopher Street to monitor his degrees of acceptable annoyance with each car, scooter, and pedestrian that cut him off. In the back, Barbara closed her eyes over his repeated braking and kept them closed—away from the traffic, Winans, and me, maybe closer to the turmoil that had landed her in the car. There was the faintest scowl in her expression as she gave her cheek over to three long fingers and wagged her pinkie slowly back and forth before her chin. Did America have spoiled princesses? She could have convinced me it did.

Then Chet made a mistake. With the Vittorio Emanuele monument of Piazza Venezia coming into view, he threw out the assumption that, however tired she must have been after her flight, she was sure to be geared up for talking to his bosses before she checked into the hotel room the embassy had arranged for her. She opened her eyes to a choice she hadn't counted on. "Actually, I wouldn't mind a shower and changing my clothes first."

Chet gave it an "Oh," then frowned at his dashboard. He was so maladroit about it that she came out sounding like a troublesome part of somebody else's schedule. And she didn't miss it. "They're not all standing around with sashes waiting for you to drive up with me, are they?"

"No, no. I just thought you'd be anxious . . ."

She sat more erectly and glanced out her window. "My brother is dead, Chet," she said evenly. "He'll be dead an hour from now, too."

That reaction I did understand.

| 7 |

THEY HAD BOOKED her into A small, neat hotel on a side street across from the Villa Borghese. I grabbed my bag from Chet's trunk while he went through a little speech about how difficult it had been even for the embassy to get a room in the place. His heavy-handedness rankled me enough to tag along into the lobby and to wait while the clerk checked Barbara off his reservation list. Then, ignoring Chet's extended hand, I sidled up to the clerk to suggest he probably had a second room for me. I wasn't surprised she kept her own counsel, pretending to be focused only on filling in the check-in form and turning over her passport. What I hadn't foreseen was that Chet would also hang back, committing himself to nothing before the clerk's dumbfounded appeal. I decided Winans had considered his duty done with his hint I look elsewhere for a room, maybe even liked the helplessness of the clerk before the insinuation that doing a favor for me was doing one for an important source of the hotel's trade. Whatever the reason, he was satisfied to stress to the clerk I was to be billed separately from Barbara and not at all to the embassy.

What my nimbleness got me was a second-floor box fronting on the Villa Borghese's ancient, chipped wall and practically hanging over the wheels of the endless motorcade turning off the Via Veneto to pass the hotel. My first sociological conclusion about Rome was that women were more likely to be driving alone than men. My second was that, stalled in the beeping and honking line down the slope of the hotel street, the women were more likely than the men to appraise the stores and pedestrians they were stuck nearby. I might have said this pointed to a natural curiosity on the part of Italian women and a natural indifference to the world on the part of Italian men if not for the small particular that the first woman leading me to this insight turned out to have German plates on her Mercedes and the second man the international **D** tag for Denmark on his Citroen. As Minton had pontificated more than one evening at The Ink, reporters who fancied themselves sociologists were always lousy at two things.

Having already worked my talents as a parasite to get a ride into the city and a hotel room only four blocks from the embassy, I had gone for the hat trick by asking Barbara to accompany her to her meeting with Chet's bosses. She had shrugged as she had about the Alitalia flight, and we had agreed to meet in the lobby within the hour. I showered, shaved, and dressed as though competing on "Beat the Clock," and got downstairs in time to sit around with the *Herald Tribune* for a good 20 minutes. I had read all the news in the *Tribune* the day before and had acted with the same anxiety about a woman going somewhere without me an existence before. Frolich, I thought, had been absolutely right about squandering the paper's money on wild goose chases.

When Barbara finally emerged from the elevator, she was wearing a snappy tan suit and matching heels. After the gray of her apartment and the black of the plane, I was beginning to get the idea that when she went for a color, she went for it all the way. "If they object to you being there, I can insist," she said, as we weaved in and out of the high noon tourists who had descended on the Veneto's sidewalk cafes.

"Let's play it by ear."

"Like Walter Wiggly."

"Who?"

"My rabbit character. Walter Wiggly always plays things by ear."

"What age group these stories for?"

"I don't want to be talking about that right now."

It was the first clang of real iron I'd heard from her, and she knew it. "I'm sorry," she said, suddenly stopping in the middle of the sidewalk.

"It's just that when people ask about my stories, they usually end up making some bad joke I've heard a hundred times. Can you understand?"

I told her I did, and didn't at all. As we descended the slope to the embassy entrance, I had my doubts "crazy" would have covered it for her if Walter Wiggly's body had been the one that had been misplaced.

Winans was waiting behind a Marine guard just inside the glass door. I caught the last few feet of his pacing and suspected the pastier color he had picked up in an hour had something to do with me. He took all of three seconds to confirm that. "This is really a meeting just for Ms. Iler," he said, directing his eyes to a spot off my left shoulder. "We're looking into a media interview at a separate time."

"I'd prefer we'd all do it together," Barbara said, so matter-of-factly and with such a deft reach into her bag for a handkerchief that it came out even more finally than her reproach to me about the children's stories. "There's nothing to hide, is there?"

Chet was getting sweatier by the second; the white shirt inside his drab gray suit looked like it was about to be sucked into his bones. "Well, let me see if Mr. King is free yet," he stammered. "I'm sure he can explain the situation better."

Winans retreated to the reception desk for the intercom phone. I looked at Barbara and saw the word SITUATION written on her forehead. Losing John Iler had been a situation from the moment Minton had told me about it, but not really. Flying first-class to Rome to find out what had happened had been a situation, but not really. Locking eyes with Barbara in her handsome tan suit and straight posture was a situation, but not really. Monochrome willowy was available on every model's runway in the world. So what was the SITUATION I saw on her forehead and that only "Mr. King" could explain to me? Suddenly, I wanted to see Mr. King more than I had wanted to see anybody in a long time.

| 8 |

CHARLES KING WAS one of those people who make you wonder if there is a genetic proclivity for growing into names. Not only did he have a massive head that wouldn't have been out of place on Simba, but the hair on his head, eyebrows, and meaty hands was much closer to tawny than blond. If he didn't have a roar to go along with everything else, he definitely played off a hulking presence capable of one.

And he needed to. Once he had extended the proper solicitousness to Barbara and a reluctant hand to me and had seated us around a glass table in his office, King had nothing to report but problems. Yes, the Nullo Borgato coffin had been shipped back to Italy, but as yet nobody had opened it to be sure Borgato was inside. Yes, the hospital where both Borgato and John Iler had died had been informed of the mix-up, but as yet the hospital mortuary hadn't completed a review of the case. And no, the Borgato family had not yet been informed of the mix-up because it remained to be confirmed officially that it was involved.

"You're suggesting there might be a third family involved?"

Because he hadn't been suggesting anything at all to *me*, had counted on both of us treating my presence only as an example of his forbearance, King took a calculated moment before saying: "I'm not implying anything of the kind. I'm merely pointing out that the body in the coffin labeled Borgato has not been re-identified officially yet." He tried to defuse his look of grievance as he turned back to Barbara. "I'm sorry the locals don't have our sense of urgency about this, but we're breathing down their necks."

She seemed on the verge of giving him the benefit of the doubt, but then he sat back with the sigh of somebody who had just completed his most ticklish assignment for the day. "If nothing's been cleared up," she said, nudging herself into annoyance, "I don't see why I had to be put on last night's plane. What exactly am I supposed to be doing while you negotiate with all these official people?"

Chet looked as eager as Barbara for an answer. "That was not our doing," King said, immediately sitting up again. "In fact, we requested that some of the technicalities be resolved before disturbing you . . ."

The man was either having a hard time relating his big title to a mortuary snafu or he had been chosen for his diplomatic post to drive Italy into the camp of Al-Qaeda. Barbara came down for the first possibility. "I'm sure these may be technicalities for you, Mr. King, but they aren't for me. All I'm asking is, when can I expect to go back with my brother's body?"

I would have enjoyed King's squirming much more if I hadn't had to think about Annie's demand for another timetable. If even lions could be transformed into weasels, what did that leave the rest of us looking like?

". . . The main thing at this point is to encourage them without being overbearing about it. They really resent that. It wouldn't be beyond them to drag their feet even more just to remind us this isn't our country."

"I've never had the illusion it was. And my brother certainly didn't."

Give King this: The more direct her shots, the more at home he looked. "Indignation has a limited value in these circumstances, Ms. Iler. Which is why we've been making appeals on more than one level. But I would also caution you—both of you—that we can accomplish much more, and far more quickly, behind the scenes than under the glare of unnecessary publicity."

"Then we have no problem," I said, figuring I wasn't going to get a better opening. "I work for a daily, and it won't go blank tomorrow if I don't file anything tonight. But by tomorrow night they might start wondering in New York if I don't send them something. So that gives us a whole afternoon, evening, morning, and another afternoon for something to get really moving behind these scenes. Right?"

Okay, I'll never be elected President or get to replace one of those Toms as Hollywood's biggest star. But sometimes you can hear the crowds roaring in your ears anyway and believe your only problem is trying to look appropriately modest before all the acclamation. I could *feel* Barbara applauding. I could *see* Chet looking impressed. I could *touch* the closed hand King had on the table and wanted to swing toward my mouth.

And that was how the first round ended. Almost.

King was already describing for Barbara the glories of the "pleasant little *trattoria*" where Chet had been charged to treat her for lunch when he stopped mid-sentence to ask if she were any relation to the children's book writer. Apparently sensing one of the trite cracks she had warned me about, she pulled in one of her long legs from under the table and admitted she was. She needn't have worried. Suddenly, King had more teeth than hair, reciting one title after another in tribute to what he called "the best baby-sitter my wife and I have ever had." There had been *Wise Owlie at the Fair, George and the Grasshoppers, Zelda the Zebra in the City* . . .

"*Zity*," she corrected, amused. "*Zelda the Zebra in the Zity.*"

"Right!" he laughed. "She gets into trouble at the zebra crossings because . . ."

"No, she gets into trouble wherever she crosses . . ."

"Because *every corner* becomes a zebra crossing!"

By the time they got to the grasshoppers, King had invited himself along to the pleasant little *trattoria*, making it clear Chet was free to find his lunch elsewhere. He didn't like giving me the name of the hospital where Nullo Borgato and John Iler had died, but decided it was a cheap enough price for not having me around as a third in the *trattoria*.

As for Barbara, she looked like she just wanted lunch, whoever her escort was going to be.

| 9 |

WITH THE HELP of Chet's plotting on a tourist map, I headed out for the hospital on foot. On the map, the building looked like it was adjacent to the Vatican, on the opposite bank of the Tiber. But because I didn't pay attention to the wide curve the river cut through the city, moving on a right-angle course from the embassy cost me a walk twice as long as necessary. Why wait for jet lag to kick in when with a little effort you can get your legs to fall off altogether?

The hospital not only had the Vatican off its right shoulder, it had once hosted the Church within its walls. My first clue was a concrete slab to the left of the entrance telling me that if I had arrived a couple of centuries earlier, I would have been visiting the Monastery of the Sacred Heart. My second clue was the sprawling fresco of angels and saints that started three-quarters up the lobby walls and that clearly continued on beyond the partitions closing off the space. Did ailing people want to see angels and saints when they gazed up from their oxygen tents? I suppose it depended on how far along they were.

For about a sentence-and-a-half, the old receptionist understood I was looking for the mortuary. Then he heard one clunky vowel too many and put down a sandwich to take a clearer look at me. "*Inglese?*"

"*Americano.*"

He nodded as though the distinction was more important to me than to him, then fanned four fingers in my face. "Four," he said emphatically. "Four. Four."

The Dottoressa Gallo was a slight woman with a big head of auburn hair and a jewelry store of bracelets hanging off both wrists. She was also the energizer rabbit who, after tiring of being merely condescending, kept calling out to her assistants for one piece of paper after another while I stumbled through my questions. Paradise for her was when her phone rang and she had a reason to slice the air with her hand, telling me to shut up. Hearing her dress down whoever was on the other end of the line at least gave me a feeling of company. I felt even better when she dropped the receiver back into the cradle with a contemptuous "*idiota!*"

"So, Iler and Borla," she said, coming back to me as though to the next ant ruining her picnic.

"Borgato. Iler and Borgato."

I liked her red face. She was apparently not used to mixing up her charges in the icebox, and even less accustomed to have her slips pointed out to her. "Well, as I'm sure your embassy has informed you, we will be expediting the identification of Signor Borgato."

Was it just my tenses? "Will be expediting?"

"It's a very complicated business."

"But don't you have Borgato's . . . ?" Blank. NYU, go to hell.

"*Impronte*? Yes, we have his fingerprints on file. Does this look like a clinic in the middle of the African jungle to you? But you don't merely snap your fingers and get things done. Believe it or not, Borgato is not my only problem right now."

I ended my agony and her impatience with what I hoped was an intelligible reminder that nobody needed her expediting more than Barbara Iler. She had a moment of graciousness—looking almost sympathetic—as she nodded. Then that moment too passed, and she was up from behind her desk with a practiced swivel for giving me the bum's rush. Then and there, my question to King about a possible third family being involved didn't occur to me.

| 10 |

I WENT TO a bar behind the hospital for a sandwich. I wolfed it down staring forlornly at the tattered directory chained to the wall under the phone. Even if the book had only one Borgato and it was the right one, I didn't want to be the one to break the news to the family. There was no way I could have carried that off smoothly in English, let alone in Italian. But I didn't want to sit around doing nothing, either, so as soon as I finished my sandwich, I looked up the paper's stringer, Fred Cleary.

Cleary looked ricketier and yellower than when he had passed through New York two years before. Walking across the Piazza Navona to the cafe where he had proposed we meet, he seemed to have to drag his bones forward to keep pace with his shoes. Sitting wasn't so easy for him, either: He had to grab both arms of the wicker chair firmly to make sure of settling without incident.

"Yeah, I know I look like shit," he said. "And no, it's not cancer or a stroke. Would you believe fucking ticks? That's what you get for going into the country—death by tick! Tick, tick, tick. Like a clock, only it's not even all that specific about the time. You know you've bought it, but you don't know when you can unwrap it. What do you think of that?"

What I thought was that Minton had been right about Cleary: The man didn't talk; he ran railroad trains with his mouth—one Pullman of a topic leading to another until the caboose told him to catch his breath.

"Of course, bizarre afflictions here are probably commonplace in New York," he said, after ordering a tea. "Tell people here about ticks and they think you got something you can take care of by burning yourself with a cigarette. And try that with some of the cigarettes they sell here! The paper burns out before you extinguish the match and then they wonder why so many people are spending extra for American, English, and South African brands. The black market here in cigarettes . . ."

After a few minutes more of this, I slipped in the Iler-Borgato mix-up; I also added the lies that Iler's sister was an old friend and I had been planning a vacation in Rome, anyway. If he suspected I was just trying to excuse Minton for not having assigned the story to him, he hid it pretty well. "I don't write much anymore," he said, using a shaking hand to light one of the Italian cigarettes he had been snorting about. "Not for newspapers, anyway. Don't pay enough and you only see about half of what you sent in print. That's if they bother sending you your piece at all, of course. Tell Minton I'm still waiting to see that series I did on the Red Brigades in 1980. You read it?"

"Before my time, Fred."

"Yeah. Well, that's when Italy was a serious place. Now you just say *euro* and they think you're a profound thinker." He took a puff, and wasn't all that wrong: A good quarter of the cigarette's paper disappeared into ash. "So how am I supposed to be useful? That's why you called, isn't it?"

I showed him the shopping list of Italian and American bureaucracies I had put together while waiting for him. Who would have signed off on the bodies along the route to New York, who should have signed off on them, who was probably now taking the heat for signing off or not signing off on them? Titles for a start, but specific names would have been better (and, I hoped, include the Dottoressa Gallo at the very top).

"Lot of detail for just helping out this friend of yours," he said, sitting back from my notebook and gingerly resetting himself against the back of his chair. "She thinking of suing? Because I'll tell you right now, Aldo Moro will rise from the dead before she collects a penny. Fuckups aren't mortal sins over here."

"No lawsuits. I just want to follow the trail."

He might have believed me, he might not have, but he abruptly reached over and tore the page out of my notebook and stuffed it in his shirt pocket. "Bet you there's more than one fuckup," he said, as the waiter set his tea in front of him. "Don't forget—this country invented dominoes."

Some book or magazine article I had once read told me he was wrong, but I saw nothing to gain by quibbling. He had enough trouble getting his bony fingers around the handle of the hot water pot and turning it over the teabag in his cup.

| 11 |

BY THE TIME I got back to the hotel, it was already after the siesta hour and I felt a step or two behind everything. My legs had gone from feeling like sandbags to feeling like barbells. Barbara had left a message in my box saying she had spoken with two teachers at the language school where her brother had worked: Was I up for going to dinner with them? Flopping down on my bed, I put a check in the Personal column (I was up for going to dinner with *her*) and a question mark in the Work column (I *should* have wanted to meet somebody who had known Iler).

Then there was this other thought to escort me into Napland: At that very moment across the Atlantic, Annie was peering into her office computer and trying to figure out which numbers didn't belong in what columns. And as she moved her mouse up and down the screen, she remembered she wouldn't have to hurry home, that the only thing waiting for her in the apartment was the box she had started filling up with my clothes. Meanwhile, I was some place where I didn't have to be rather than in a place where I soon wouldn't be. Iler and Borgato suddenly didn't seem like the only misplaced bodies. There were, in fact, so many of them that I was beginning to lose count.

| 12 |

JOHN ILER'S FELLOW-TEACHERS were Mark St. Cyr and Claire
Pettit. St. Cyr was a small, twitchy guy who kept an empty pipe in his
mouth as he shook hands with Barbara and expressed his condolences.
Pettit was a chubby, freckled redhead who immediately scolded St. Cyr
for "saying what a thousand other people have probably been saying to
her lately." Even before we had moved away from our rendezvous point
at the Campo de' Fiori, the two of them were into the first of what would
be several hissy-fit exchanges. Before we got to a *trattoria* a couple of
blocks away, I had made him out as a closet gay who went trolling under
protection and her as Ms. Low Self-Esteem grateful for the role he had
given her.

Naturally, I was almost completely wrong. St. Cyr was gay, but he
wasn't in the least timid about declaring it. When his pipe or fork wasn't
in his mouth, he had one tart tale after another to offer about this one
he'd had, that one he wouldn't have minded having, or that other one
who had as much chance of having him as the next Russian tsar did. For
counterpoint, Pettit threw in reminders of two ex-lovers who had found
St. Cyr to be a creep, her own ex-husband who had theorized that the
creep was also a eunuch, and her jolly attempts to disprove that with a
series of friends of both sexes (snort, giggle, snort).

So what did Barbara and I do when we weren't rolling our eyes at each
other? I concentrated on the restaurant's thick white wine, also throwing

in a thought or two about the significance of her breaking her single-color dress code by wearing a black-and-green striped shirt. She had the more arduous task of trying to glean some information about Johnny—how her brother had been feeling immediately before his attack, had he been considered a good English teacher by his Italian students, how well had they known each other. For a while, she might as well have been asking that next tsar. Neither St. Cyr nor Pettit had socialized much with Johnny, he had always been "friendly but standoffish," they had never heard any complaints about him at the school. But then one question too many about Johnny Iler's gifts in a classroom brought a sniffled laugh from St. Cyr. "Well, he didn't really have to be all that good at it, anyway, did he?"

Barbara's expression said she had heard what I had: Some idiom or phrase in Italian she didn't understand. Except that St. Cyr was speaking English.

"I don't think it's any secret," Pettit put in. "Everybody in the school knew Johnny was working for the government."

I didn't know why Barbara was looking at me: I was back in Minton's office being handed an assignment that was about to turn into another Irangate, Watergate, or just plain Ilergate. "Where did you get such an idea?" she asked Heckle and Jeckle.

Neither St. Cyr nor Pettit looked unsure. "Obviously, you didn't see him much lately," he said, spearing a tomato slice with the sinuous hauteur of someone who had long ago come to regard tomatoes as inferior commodities. "But you can tell who's a spook and who isn't. As long as we were talking about students or the curriculum or something like that, Johnny was fine. But he never wanted to talk about himself. And forget about being invited to his apartment!"

"There's no question," Pettit nodded to her plate. "He was leading a double life. The teaching was just a front."

That should have done it. We should have motioned to the waiter, insisted on paying the bill for so much helpful information, then fled from Heckle and Jeckle faster than roadrunners. But then Pettit worked up an additional frown for Barbara. "But why don't you talk to Alicia about all that? I'm sure she knows more about it than we do."

Personally, I would have preferred Jovanka or Fatima, but Barbara looked stumped enough by Alicia. "The one he was living with," Pettit prodded. "Wasn't that her name, Mark?"

"You mean you haven't talked to Alicia?" St. Cyr asked, matching his partner's disapproval. "Haven't you been over to his place? I assumed she was the one who told you he'd died."

"No, that came from the embassy," she said lamely. "The hospital must've informed them."

For the briefest of moments, I could understand the reactions of St. Cyr and Pettit. It wasn't the spookiness over Walter Wiggly on the Via Veneto; this was a more passive brand. Even without an Ilergate in the offing, there was something unnerving about her stupor before the thought of a Johnny Iler girlfriend.

"How would I find this woman?" she managed.

Pettit answered with what seemed like spiteful speed: hauling her shoulder bag up from the floor, pulling out an address book, and assuming the dictation position. I jotted down the name and telephone number in my notebook, then stuck it back into my pocket before Barbara had to look enthusiastic about accepting it.

"The only reason I know her name is because I had to call Johnny once about switching classes," Pettit said. "Naturally, she was another big secret he never wanted to share with anybody. You can bet whatever he was really up to, she was up to it with him."

Barbara nodded dumbly. I thought that an intelligent reaction.

| 13 |

EVEN WITH BARBARA'S self-absorption in the taxi on the way back to the hotel, I had plenty of company. Most of all, there was Wally Masterson and my ability to believe anything if I wanted to badly enough. Masterson had been with the graphics department when I had joined the paper—a 50ish artist with a monk's gray tonsure for hair and a Southern twang who seemed to spend an hour every shift punching on keys for aligning photographs and the next six belting scotches downstairs at The Ink. The veterans at the paper had all but established a pool on when he would be fired, jump out a window, or simply be found drunk, dead, or both under a bus. That had been enough for me to climb on a stool next to him one night, and he had repaid the gesture a dozen times over by telling me, in encyclopedic detail, why I shouldn't waste my time with any artist except Cezanne because "'The Card Players' is why some people belong on earth and why most don't."

That relatively sane misanthropy had ended with the arrival of The Chief. One night, Masterson had been into one of his usual tirades against the Ops and Pops of the art world, I had mumbled something apprecia-tive of his viewpoint, and he had reared back on his stool to study me through some distant lens and then pronounce: "The Chief likes you, Danny." The Chief, it turned out, was the Lakota sitting between us at the bar—visible to nobody but Wally Masterson, but a severe guardian who rarely approved of the people he frequented.

On one level, everything had gone downhill from there. Sal the bar-tender and a couple of people at the paper had already been introduced to The Chief, and they had gradually passed the word until somebody in the graphics department was calling somebody in personnel and some-body in personnel was calling medical. Wally Masterson had ended up in Bellevue, where he was to linger for a couple of years before succumbing to a stroke. The other level, as far as I was concerned, had been the hour or more at The Ink that evening when Masterson, The Chief, and I had examined the world's problems together. Of course, the guy had been delusional. Of course, I had been humoring him. Of course, I had been sad he had deteriorated so far from once-upon-a-time ambitions to be worthy of his master Cezanne. But the fact was, I had also been *conversa-tional*—ready to accept The Chief in Masterson's description of him with his Venetian blind chest protector and austere expression, wondering on some far side of reason if maybe there *had been* somebody there. Was it really so bad to think some people could get along with the invisible as well as the visible? Jimmy Stewart had been charming with *Harvey*, hadn't he? And what about those even older Topper movies? All they had shown was people tripping over hassocks or walking into closed doors. Why should Wally Masterson be considered any more dangerous?

All by way of saying that when we got back to the hotel bar, I wasn't quite as dismissive of Johnny Iler, CIA Agent, as I might have been. That certainly jibed with Iler's mysterious project, didn't it? Barbara? She wasn't sure—about that, about Alicia, about anything at all except Heckle and Jeckle. "Damn right they weren't close to Johnny," she fumed as soon as she sipped her brandy. "Have you ever met such crawly people?"

I thought of the manager of my neighborhood laundromat who had gained the nickname T.C. (Today's Catch) because of his throbbing oys-ter of a left eye but knew she didn't want to hear about him. Instead, I asked what I had to ask; whether it was Ed Minton or Wally Masterson, I was still on assignment. "He ever hint at anything to you that wouldn't make that such a ridiculous idea?"

"God knows somebody with his brains was doing more than teach-ing the verb *to be*, but he couldn't have passed a physical to work for the post office, let alone some hush-hush government thing. But can you imagine people learning English from those two tonight?"

Clearly, she didn't want to spend any more thoughts on John Iler, Secret Agent. "Maybe that's what they're good at," I said, deciding to retire Ilergate for the night. "Everybody's good at something. Some little expertise that exists despite their personalities. Maybe their students just have to listen to them about pronouns and conjugations, and they're really brilliant at that."

"Why don't I believe it?"

My shrug took too long. Suddenly it was what I thought *I* was good at despite my personality. My hesitation felt so wonderfully moody and cosmopolitan in my European surroundings that when the bartender asked if we wanted refills, how could we have said no?

She pinched an invisible fold out of her black slacks and looked brave to be facing me again. "Why am I attracted to you?"

I told myself the hot spear in my lungs was self-inflicted; why set myself up for a fall? "The booze."

"No."

"You're adrift. Over here, probably since you heard about Johnny."

She smiled tightly; a weariness she wasn't sure she had earned. "Maybe further back than that."

Even Julius Caesar had stopped after the first couple of transparent bluffs, but I didn't. "People like Heckle and Jeckle bother you."

Boom! I might as well have taken the laurel held out to me and put a match to it. "Yes, they do," she said, back in the outside world that wasn't attracted to me. "Johnny shouldn't have ended up working with people like that. I *prefer* to think he was some kind of spy. He was really a brilliant man. Languages alone—he spoke Italian, French, Spanish, even a little Portuguese. And science—god, if he'd had any discipline at all, there's no telling what he would have accomplished. He shouldn't have just been teaching 'Where is the Passport Office?' with those two."

"But he wasn't. He had this secret project you said."

She nodded, but not all that confidently, and I suddenly wondered whether Iler's fan club—his sister and Heckle and Jeckle—wasn't made up of people who simply didn't want to believe he *had been* good only for 'Where is the Passport Office?'. The trouble with that thought, of course, was that it meant I would have to go back to thinking of him only as a mislaid corpse.

"What would Wise Owlie have said?"

She tapped a fingernail against her glass to be sure. "He would have said I gave you the perfect opening to say how much you're attracted to me, too, but you haven't taken it."

"Sorry. I took my vibes for granted."

"Don't."

As soon as I took her hand and kissed it, smelling her hand lotion, we both knew we weren't ready to go any further that night. We were promising each other, reassuring each other, guaranteeing each other, but we weren't puncturing the cellophane shield between us—not yet. We could have, and as easily as leaving a tip and walking over to the elevator, but there was all that *physicality* waiting upstairs. Who wanted to make it so finite so fast?

| 14 |

WAS IT ME or Charles King and the weight of the United States of America with all its dollars, nuclear missiles, and international box-office hits? I preferred thinking it was me. Chet Winans called Barbara the next morning to say the hospital had checked the fingerprints of the body inside Nullo Borgato's coffin and had confirmed that Nullo Borgato had indeed been the brief visitor to Kennedy Airport. Winans said "the hospital," but I had a much nicer picture of the Dottoressa Gallo waiting for me to leave her office, then rushing over to an *idiota* on her staff and screaming: "This is terrible, this is terrible! The newspapers in America are going to make a mockery of me! Get that print check done and right now! We must placate that reporter before it is too late!"

With Borgato's body identified, I had no more problems about contacting the family. Well, one. There turned out to be 38 Borgatos in the book. Did I go through them one by one asking if they had recently had a death in the family? Did I ask for help from Cleary, who was already doing something for me? Or did I go to King, who wouldn't want to do anything for me? No, no, and no answers left only Chet Winans.

"It'd really be a help, Chet," I said into his second-long silence at the other end of the line. "We're not talking about official secrets here, right?"

When you're hot, you're hot. I heard some shuffling of paper, then: "We have only a son—Antonino Borgato, known as Nino. In Trastevere.

He has some kind of coffee house or something. There's an ex-wife, too, but she doesn't live in Rome. It's the son you have to talk to."

With that, my day began to fill out. Trastevere with Nino Borgato, then the Piazza Navona with Cleary to find out what he had dug up. Sometime before nightfall, I also expected to go with Barbara to her brother's apartment, maybe even meet the Alicia whose existence made her so jumpy. So much to call Minton about and so little time to do it!

| 15 |

WINANS HAD SAID coffee house and had meant coffee house—not as in Italian bar or cafe, but as in San Francisco beatnik, wormholed tables, blue ceiling lights for the wannabe blind, free circulation magazine racks, bloated middle-aged guys and scrawny-armed women sitting over mugs and reading while Parker and Monk played the familiar anthems. But for all its painstaking nostalgia, the place hadn't quite squeezed its rear end and legs into the time warp. There was just too much unaffected Roman shouting blowing through the front door from the open-air market across the street and even more interference from a soap opera on the TV above the coffee machines. A pregnant blonde watching the set also kept time in its place by keeping up a muttering monologue with the characters she was following.

Nino Borgato was around 30, with a weak face and braying swagger I had last seen in the son of a racketeer at a criminal trial. Except Nino didn't have two ex-boxers for bodyguards to escort him back and forth from a limousine to the courtroom. What he did have was a long line on how he was never going to get rich serving an *espresso* every half-hour and watching a customer take an hour to drink it, how his wife (the blonde behind the counter) had been pregnant three times in four years, and how his father hadn't left him a single penny in his will. So . . . . . .

"You know how much it costs to dig up a grave?"

"I have no idea."

"A lot. Who's going to pay for it? You? This dead American's sister?"

"The hospital or some government agency, I'm sure."

He took in my answer with disappointment: Somewhere in his slack jaw and sharp eyes, he had been hurriedly adding up numbers for bilking Barbara or me. "But you don't even know for sure if this American is in my father's grave."

"It's very likely, isn't it? And what do you care about digging it up, anyway? The main thing for your family is your father's body is back at the mortuary, right?"

"I don't like that place," he said, as though that answered something.

I tried the tack I had that first meeting with Barbara. "Did your father have a sense of humor?"

"You mean would he find this *casino* funny? Yeah. He'd think of it as more of the same. His life was a fuckup, so why shouldn't his death be?"

It wasn't until I had filled up almost three pages of details about Nullo Borgato that I told Nino I had enough. Later on, I gave myself a lot of reasons for having let him go on. I had liked seeing him lose his sneer, sound almost vulnerable, about his father. I had liked being able to grasp the thrust of all his tales, bless you, NYU. I had liked reminding myself that my story might have been about two misplaced bodies, but that two *people* had also once been inside those bodies. But most of all, as I admitted to myself crossing back over the Tiber on my way to see Fred Cleary, I had liked Nullo Borgato. He appealed to me even more than John Iler, 007.

To hear Nino, his father had been Renaissance Man—if the Renaissance had been a vast array of blue-collar trades and hustles and if the man had found a way to create fiascos in all of them. Earnestness and ambition? Nullo Borgato had apparently minted those qualities—and had their molten metals immediately spill over his feet. As a teenager, he had been a middleweight boxer who had lied convincingly enough about his age to have his left ear damaged beyond repair after only four bouts. Happily, and unhappily for him, his grit had come to the attention of some mildly important thug, who had given him a job twisting the arms and breaking the kneecaps of welching gamblers. This career had come to an end when one of the welchers turned out to be a police captain trained in the martial arts, leaving Borgato with a bad back to go along with his bad ear. Then there had been something else about contraband cigarettes and another something about smuggled diamonds (okay, so I didn't get *every* word). According to Nino, none of this had led to jail time, but there had been the equivalent of a prison sentence in all the time the old man had spent at police stations answering questions and lining up against a wall for witnesses.

Then Nullo Borgato had hit the higher road. He had met Nino's mother, a civil servant at the Education Ministry and a Communist Party activist. She had helped him get a job in the Post Office—a recommendation she had regretted sorely for the first few months. On one occasion, Nullo had cancelled an entire day's worth of mail with an inkless machine; another time he had dropped a lighted cigarette into a bin full of overseas packages; a third time he had slugged a customer for ignoring a line behind him and insisting on stamping his letters right at the window. Such episodes, Nino said, had been conversational fodder at the dinner table—in anger when his mother had been on the warpath, as drollery when his father had gotten into a nah-nah-nah spitting contest with some old friend. But Nullo Borgato had survived them, mainly thanks to the fact that he had been taken under the wing of a Party middleshot at the Post Office who had shuffled him from task to task until he had compiled too much seniority to be fired. And 28 years later, he had taken his pension buyout as one of the most popular employees in the history of his substation.

And even that had been only part of it. Nullo Borgato had nurtured bigger dreams than selling stamps efficiently. Spurred on by his wife, he had taken night writing courses, becoming a regular contributor to the Post Office newsletter and a relentless correspondent with newspapers and magazines that had offended his political views. Unfortunately for him, he had signed more than one of his letters with his title as the substation's Party cell secretary, and the Communist bureaucrats hadn't always been happy having him represent their position. This had apparently led to an escalating series of warnings, censures, and suspensions—and to another theater of battle with his wife, who had had her own aspirations in the regional ranks of the Party.

"Then he ran into the opera singer," Nino said, the pout back on his face. "She was like you—she didn't have any money, either."

"All very interesting. But this is really outside the area I'm reporting on . . ."

And I made it all the way out of the coffee house and down to the Ponte Garibaldi. It was only as I was passing the ruins of Largo Argentina that I admitted the theme of the morning wasn't what a great beating heart I was for having let Nino Borgato ramble on about his father, but why I had cut him off when I had: *I couldn't stand anymore!* Between whom John Iler might have been and whom Nullo Borgato had been, there was an awfully familiar face. Between the fanciful and the futile, where there should have been only a couple of properly marked caskets, there was Ed Minton's favorite roving reporter. I saw him as clearly as I had once seen The Chief standing next to me at The Ink.

| 16 |

FRED CLEARY WAS sitting at the same table in the Piazza Navona where we had sat the day before, and again had a cup of tea in front of him. He still looked like he had staggered away from a plane crash, but he also seemed to have taken new stock of his body parts. In short, he no longer believed I had just happened into the Borgato-Iler mess because of some old friend.

"I was never the worst scenter on the trail," he prodded.

"Anything you can help me with, Fred, you get full credit for. Money, byline, whatever."

"The former would be more helpful than the latter. They don't even wrap the fish bones in yesterday's bylines anymore. Recycling has cost us all a little romance, don't you think?"

"What did you get?"

He pulled a sheaf of papers out of his pocket I didn't want to see. A, he had done too much work for just the couple of names I wanted and would expect to be paid accordingly. B, Nino Borgato's tales about his father had been enough overdrive on the morning for a simple corpse story.

"Nobody at Ciampino Airport checks anything but the manifest, and there was no second manifest for Iler. So you can rule out Borgato getting sent to New York and Iler to Milan or some other place because they screwed up at the airport."

"I never thought that was a possibility."

"Oh? Why?"

"Because Borgato's from here."

He nodded as though that were a reasonable objection. "So the mix-up took place before the airport."

"With you all the way."

"Okay, now here's where it gets interesting. Three people died in that hospital that day. Borgato, Iler . . ."

I knew the third name without waiting for Cleary to control his trembling fingers over his papers. "Borla," I said, picturing the Dottoressa Gallo's red face.

He was as impressed as he should have been, and I toasted myself by flagging down a waitress for a Bloody Mary. "The mortuary chief made a slip," I finally said to him. "Maybe it's an occupational hazard to think of the deceased as sets according to the day."

"Did she also tell you there's no record of this Borla's body being picked up?"

What should have occurred to me at that moment—and which in true *esprit de l'escalier* fashion did later on—was that Cleary wasn't suffering from a tick bite, but from some alien surgical procedure. He had such a triumphant glow in his eyes that I might have been one of those soon-to-get-his skeptics in the first scene of "The X Files." "I guess you have a point here, right?"

"That might not even be Borgato in the casket! It could be this Lamberto Borla!"

He was taken aback when I told him about the positive identification, but not completely defeated. "Why would they take the hospital's word for it? That's where the whole fuckup started."

"Maybe they just want to keep things simple, Fred. This one that's supposed to be there is here, so the one that's supposed to be here is probably there."

"I don't trust it. This is the country . . ."

"I know. Dominoes. But all I really want to know at this point are the names of the little elves along the conveyor belt. This one put Borgato on the wrong . . ."

He snatched at the papers to find a name. "Alicia Silvestri," he barked. "She got the ball rolling by signing off on Iler and having the hospital call the embassy."

That made sense, so much so it seemed incredible nobody had mentioned it before. And not only not to me. Somewhere along the line— say, in the first phone call from the embassy to East 84th Street, or out at the Kennedy Airport hangar, or, failing all else, in the middle of Charles King's effusions over lunch about *Zelda the Zebra in the Zity*—Barbara should have heard about Alicia Silvestri before Heckle and Jeckle had sprung the woman on her.

"Where did you get all this stuff?"

Cleary had been waiting for that question for 24 hours. "It's my territory," he said smartly. "You don't get people to trust you just by speaking their language. You have to convince them you've got some of the same long-haul interests they do. Remember the old westerns where the hero had to live with the Indians before they began to trust him? I don't mean that Kevin Costner shit. That was so touchy-feely I wanted to puke. I mean like Richard Harris in that . . . ."

I had a feeling I should have been angry about something, but I wasn't sure what. There suddenly seemed to be too many candidates and not enough of them. Instead, I invited Cleary—and his sheaf of papers— to lunch. It seemed like the most amiable way of finding out what else I should have been doing all along.

| 17 |

BARBARA WAS BACK to her black dress for her brother's apartment. In the cab, she was also back to the edginess she had shown walking to the embassy the day before. "Alicia sounded very nice on the phone," she reassured me a second time as we maneuvered miraculously around a tram. "She knew nothing about all the confusion."

"Why should she? Once she told the hospital what to do, she just assumed everything would work out."

She gave away nothing, just grabbed her roof strap more firmly as the driver swerved around another cab. I thought about the conversation I was going to have to have with Minton in about six hours.

*"Remember **Shock Corridor**, Ed?"*

"What the hell's that?"

"An old movie where this writer gets himself checked into a loony bin so he can do an investigative report from the inside. Of course, nobody believes he's faking it all and he ends up really going nuts."

"What's that got to do with anything?"

"Iler's crazy sister. She's got this real emotional problem with her brother; doesn't want to believe he ever had a lover. Blotted out this woman completely."

"Yeah? So?"

"So I'm attracted to this crazy sister and all her animal characters. And that's where I'm going to end up, too—completely in her world."

"You wish."

I hadn't thought so. But if I could be assured of being surrounded by Special Agent John Iler, Nullo Borgato the educated thug, and Lamberto Borla the Body Fred Cleary Said Should Have Been Traced, why not aspire to Danny the Dandy Panda? It sure as hell beat flying back to New York and seeing my marriage years packed into a couple of Dannon boxes.

| 18 |

OUR DESTINATION TURNED out to be an eight-floor high-rise of almost as many balconies as windows. Barbara showed nothing at the names SILVESTRI-ILER on the bell, but their order and the fact that the apartment was on the top floor told me Alicia Silvestri had gained top billing because she had more income than an English language teacher. Going up in the elevator, I wondered if she had been one of the moths drawn to the flame of Iler's "I'm sick, I'm dying" routine or if she had originally been assigned to run him by Langley and, between their orders to terminate rogue agents with prejudice, had fallen in love with him. It didn't seem like speculation to share with Barbara. She was busy enough not puncturing her purse with her fingernails.

Alicia Silvestri was waiting for us in her doorway. She was a small, frumpy woman with graying hair, closer to 50 than to 40. She stepped out into the hallway to hug Barbara expansively, then clasped my hand as the answer to some briefer prayer. The excuse for Barbara that I would be needed as an interpreter evaporated immediately: Alicia Silvestri spoke English fluently.

She led us into a big sun-lighted room with gleaming maroon tiles and no carpets. A couple of sofas and easy chairs around a coffee table looked barely used; the walls, on the other hand, were completely used. They amounted to a small museum of paintings—from framed miniatures to matted canvasses three feet high, hung so slapdash next to one another they didn't seem to be there for viewing so much as for just announcing their existence. A glare through the French windows made it hard to see details in most of them, but the couple I could make out were naïf versions of tiny folk creatures—dwarfs, gremlins, trolls—peering out from behind lush green foliage and the reddest of redwoods. I assumed Alicia Silvestri was the painter.

"I know you are not English," she said, bustling off deeper into the apartment as soon as she had sat us on one of the sofas, "but I always liked the custom of tea at this hour. I will be right back."

Barbara looked like she needed Alicia's run into the kitchen to count off her wins and losses—and to figure out which was which. The woman was older than Iler by a good decade, should not have worn lime bolero pants that accented her big ass, and might have closed the top button of her denim shirt to cover her frayed bra. She might have been a little more formal at the door, not presuming Barbara accepted her as family. She might have offered a choice of beverages instead of ramming her Anglophilia down our throats. She might have let us select our own chairs instead of confining us to the one sofa like two Jehovah's Witnesses invited in to explain our God. She might have . . .

"I'm an idiot, right, Danny?"

She might as well have been accusing me. "They compare actors for Oscars. Why should you be different?"

Alicia returned with a tea set and a plate of *biscotti* on a wooden tray. "I know, I should have a silver tray," she said, taking the single chair opposite us. "Johnny always said that. But this is from Sri Lanka, and they know about tea down there as much as anyone."

Sri Lanka reminded us of Ceylon, Thailand of Siam, and Russia of the USSR. All of them—with Iran and Myanmar to come, I was sure—reminded me of the Jovanka or Fatima with the cat eyes and *double entendres* I had been looking forward to meeting. Then Barbara spoiled all the jollity by mentioning Iler. "I was always in competition with you," Alicia said with the bright look she had maintained since the door. "And now I can see why. You must have been . . . No, not a model. You have to be foolish to be a model and you don't look foolish. I know! One of those contest women for being beautiful! You don't do it for a profession. You are just on the beach one day, someone comes up to you with a camera, and *voila*! You win without making an effort. Your grace wins it for you."

"Did it make me rich?"

Alicia waved her hand so dismissively she almost knocked the cup off her saucer. "Money, money, money. You know when I stopped worrying about money?"

"When you had some?"

She wasn't quite as sure she had prayed for me, even the least bit. "When I had something else to worry about," she corrected me. "When my work all started to look the same. When I was ill and wasn't sure I would get better. Then when Johnny got sick. When you worry about money, it is because you have nothing else to worry about. Give people something else to think about, that's the solution."

"And the money will just come?"

"Absolutely."

Barbara literally squirmed away from our philosophical discussion to sit higher. "I was hoping you could tell me something about Johnny," she said. "How he got sick, what happened."

"I'm not sure how much there is to tell. Maybe all of us leave less of an impression on others than we hope. What do you think?"

"How long was he sick?"

Alicia sipped her tea slowly; not to gain time to remember, it looked, but to block a rush of unwanted memory. "Two days," she said finally. "He couldn't get up from bed. Tuesday of last week, I think. He said his head felt strange, very light, he wasn't strong enough to stand up. I don't have a car, so I asked Signor Perrone, our neighbor across the hall, to drive us to the hospital. Have a *biscotto*. They are very good."

"They couldn't do anything in the hospital?"

"I heard one of them in the Emergency Room say he would not survive until the morning. About that they were wrong! He lasted two days! Johnny was tougher than they thought!"

Barbara looked so skeptical Alicia immediately reconsidered. "No, he wasn't tough at all," she smiled wanly. "But I have been saying that to a lot of people the last few days. You knew him better, of course."

Barbara took a *biscotto*.

After some minutes of Iler's final hours in bed, I thought I had enough diplomatic room to stand up for a closer inspection of the paintings on the walls. Not just the ones I had glimpsed walking in, but almost every one of them featured elves, dwarfs, and the like in some woodland, near a stream, or on a mountain. The meticulousness was of a jewel cutter: figures barely centimeters high had distinct eyebrows and different shaped buckles on their shoes. In some of the paintings, she had clustered as many as a dozen little people around a rock or a tree branch, each with his personally colored cap and hat. In one sense, it was *Where's Waldo?* driven to an extreme. But there was more than the coyness of comics going on; in canvas after canvas, big, small, or medium, the elaborateness of everything overwhelmed specific colors, shapes, and figures. I recognized what I was looking at, but not quite.

"No, you haven't seen them before," she called out behind me.

"How do you know?"

"You've seen figures *like* them, paintings *like* them. They remind you of Snow White or Aesop or the Grimm Brothers. But those pieces illustrate *my* stories and those you don't know."

She tittered to take the edge off her haughty pronouncement, and I sat back down again before I distracted her any longer from the only one of her stories Barbara wanted to hear. As she went back to Iler's hospital stay, I decided I didn't like her, then decided I did, then decided it was irrelevant to both of us which side I came down on her loopiness. Even in her effort to keep reigned in for the first meeting with her lover's family, she was evidently that close to slipping back into a more comfortable extravagance. She wore garish pants and frayed underwear? Your problem. She talked without thinking and sometimes admitted she didn't know what the hell she was talking about? Your problem. She had been mothering a much younger neurotic? Your problem. Somebody somewhere along the line had pointed out to her that Iler had undoubtedly seen some relationship between her leprechauns and all the Wise Owlies of Barbara's mind? Deal with it. Everybody lived in a glass house, and she didn't waste time pricing the land under it. All she really had time for was completing another picture that, framed and hung, might make her just a little less visible to outsiders. The paintings weren't crowding the walls to be viewed *or* to announce their own existence, I decided on my second pass; dwarf by dwarf, they were being piled up to block out hers.

"So this teaching job was just because it was there?" Barbara asked, looking more pained with every particular Alicia surrendered.

"Why not? Johnny wasn't very good in Italian, but they had a method at this place where you speak English from the first class. What else was he supposed to do? Johnny wasn't exactly a genius. The only thing I ever saw him upset about was his crossword puzzles. He would get very annoyed if he didn't know the name of some bird in Indonesia. Such nonsense!"

Barbara was so furious she aimed her stare all the way across the living room, toward another painting on the dividing wall to a dining room. I looked for some sign of dissembling in Alicia Silvestri's expression. The obvious answer, of course, was that Iler had been such a genius that he had even hoodwinked his lady friend into believing he had been a cipher.

| 19 |

"BE A LOT better if the son of a bitch was selling nuclear parts to the Terrorist Brotherhood or something." Minton was speaking so lowly I wondered if Frolich wasn't standing right outside his office.

I could have hedged my bets, quoted Heckle and Jeckle, but I didn't want to. There should have been worthier ways of prolonging my sabbatical. "Well, he wasn't. He was a language teacher with a bad heart who lived with an Italian painter hung up on dwarfs and trolls. Tell the truth, he sounds like that Peter Sellers guy in *Being There*. A blank slate."

"Swell. So you'll be coming home tomorrow, right?"

I looked around my hotel room to see if any representative of the Bullshit Police was listening in. I didn't see anybody. "There might be a third body, Ed."

"You're kidding! An American?"

In for a penny, in for the whole euro. "I should know tomorrow."

Minton fell silent, and I could picture Frolich stepping into his office and gesturing for a moment of his time. "This wouldn't just be angling for a few more pastas, would it?" he came back.

"You know these government offices, Ed. Everything is *domani* just because that's not today."

He didn't believe me any more than I did, and he found that funny. "What I know, sport, is I'm counting on you for lots of inches. Measure them by the Citi Field foul lines. I want something tomorrow. *Ciao*."

I put the receiver down into my least favorite question: NOW WHAT? Everything that occurred to me was a half, a partial, a fraction, of what it might have been. I could have taken up Cleary's invitation at lunch to join him for drinks at the Foreign Press Club; but who wanted to be with Fred Cleary more than once a day? I could have followed up on my promise to Nino Borgato to drop back at the coffee house and hear more about his father and the American opera singer; but I had already indulged that romance long enough. I could have waited for Barbara to make up her mind about whether she wanted to go out for dinner; but I was beginning to feel needy for her company, and that was far too premature to be reassuring for either of us. I could have even called Alicia Silvestri and told her I was accepting the dinner invitation she had extended before we had left her place; but, with no spook tales for a payoff, why did I want to hear more about John Iler or the moronic masses that worried about money?

I gave myself a half-hour truce by looking at the clips on Iler's death Cleary had gathered for me. Or more accurately, I spent 25 minutes on trying to follow a TV documentary on marble foundries and 3 minutes on glancing at the two Italian papers that had bothered to carry the same three-line agency dispatch on the "*professore americano*" who had died in his hospital bed. When you're sour, you're sour: What I concluded from my research was that Johnny Iler hadn't been all that interesting even as a filler. Blank slate, I had told Minton? Even that seemed like an exaggeration.

I switched to a dubbed Goldie Hawn movie. Something about a creepy husband who was supposed to be dead but who was actually trying to kill her. I could have done without the associating, but I suddenly found myself thinking of the first time I had seen Annie. It had been a jammed Long Island basement, a Saturday night party thrown by a guy named Patterson I had since lost touch with. I had been sitting in a corner with a beer wondering why Patterson still had Christopher Cross records when she had appeared from between bodies to get to the potato chips on the table next to me. She had been wearing red-heeled sandals, a mandarin kind of blue dress, and a protective smile against either what somebody had just said to her or what somebody might someday say to her. Then she had been bumped from behind and had landed on my lap. We had both giggled. She had introduced herself. I had introduced myself. She hadn't been in a hurry to adjust the hemline that had gone up one knee almost mid-thigh, and I hadn't been in one to move the leg that had begun losing circulation the moment she had collapsed on it. How much less effort could we have put into falling into each other?

Well, maybe in one way, I realized: I hadn't used Johnny Iler's gambit in telling her how close I was to death's door.

Then my phone rang, and Chet Winans wanted to know if I had anything going for dinner. I hated sounding so available.

| 20 |

I KNEW WHAT Winans was up to before he picked me up in front of the hotel and drove us over to a Tuscan restaurant behind the Pantheon. I'd dealt with enough flacks and lawyers in New York to sense when the besieged considered it useful to send out a scouting party to see where the attack was going to come from and if it could still be headed off. I didn't care. Even Chet's eager-to-please company seemed better than being alone with old Goldie Hawn movies.

The restaurant was a dimly lighted igloo with a strong aroma of cold cuts in the air. I wasn't aware until after we had sat down in the back and Winans began whispering that we had walked past a deputy prime minister, a couple of senators, and the star of a TV quiz show. I didn't have to act impressed; I was immediately ordered not to. "I know, I know. You never heard of any of them. It's not like walking into some New York place and seeing David Letterman. But it's pretty big stuff here."

"Letterman and I don't go to the same restaurants, Chet."

"Well, you know what I mean."

"I think so. You patronize A by sounding in awe of B when you really want to patronize B because you know he deserves it as much as A."

I smiled so he'd know it was a friendly crack. "Maybe I'm in awe of all of them," he smiled back.

"Probably not as much as you want me to believe."

If nothing else, he called it quits trying to impress both of us with our surroundings. But he had barely ordered the wine and pate before he made his first probe. "Now that Borgato's been identified, the Italians have guaranteed they'll dig up Iler tomorrow."

"*Domani?*"

"No, they mean it. They don't need negative publicity, either."

"Who's the 'either?'"

"I know what you're thinking. We should've checked the casket before it left Italy."

"It never occurred to me that was part of your job."

"But however you write it, it's going to look like we should've done that. The Negligent Bureaucracy versus The Bereaved Sister. Okay, that's legit. But it'd be nice if you could also squeeze in there how much we've been doing behind the scenes."

"The wine's not even here yet, and you know all about how I'm going to write this."

"Am I that far off?"

He was, Then and there I wanted to write about Johnny Iler as briefly as the Italian news agency had. I had nothing more to say. Even if I had toyed with more than a corpse story, the two women in Iler's life had, in different ways, said I was just going to come up with a *living* corpse story. No wonder they had preferred the company of Wise Owlie and forest trolls!

The wine came and kept coming. There was the pate and then a *fiorentina* between glasses, but they were mainly fuel for opening another bottle. Winans lost his official wariness, first to sound apologetic again for Wilkes-Barre and the Phillies, then to confess his envy of friends who had gone to Penn State while he had shuffled through four years of St. Joseph's and Rolling Rock in Philadelphia. Then he got *really* irritating.

"I wonder how Barbara's doing with the Kings and their Parioli friends . . . Oh, she didn't tell you? There was no way Charlotte, that's Mrs. King, was going to let her favorite children's author get out of Rome without inviting her to dinner . . ."

While he went on about Charlotte King's artichoke dips and dippy circle, I looked at the problem from all analytic angles. Only one scenario seemed possible. Barbara had known about the invitation since her lunch with King, meaning she had blindsided me not only with her procrastination about going out together for dinner, but even last night in the hotel bar after seeing Heckle and Jeckle. She wouldn't have resorted to such a deceit if I hadn't been making her edgy. Winans calling me had been King's insurance policy against her deciding at the last minute to drag me along for the artichoke dip.

Why did that scenario pinch even in its flattery?

Answer: For the exact same reasons I had given her at the hotel bar. Because I had drunk too much wine. Because I was adrift. Because I was surrounded by too many Chets. And then—and maybe only then—because I was attracted to her.

By the time we got out of the restaurant, Chet was too wobbly to get behind a wheel, and knew it. But he wasn't about to let somebody without an international license take him home, either. "I'll just leave it here," he said, making several gropes for a shopping bag he had left in the back seat of the car, "and pick it up tomorrow. We try to discourage scandal among embassy employees. Now it's time for a nightcap."

Leaving his car reinvigorated him. As we trudged up to the Corso to look for a taxi, he opened a new can of Wilkes-Barre stories, and this one was all local pride—the racetrack where his father had worked all his life, the symphony orchestra that had featured a Winans in the string section for generations. Worse, he became more critical of my drivel. "Why would you have expected Iler to be interesting, in the first place?" he asked, as we barreled along the Tiber to some nightclub he knew about. "Maybe the only time he's interesting is now, when he's dead and lost."

"You shouldn't say that of anybody."

"You mean I shouldn't say it about the brother of Barbara Iler. You remember—the one with legs up to her tits? That's who you're thinking about. If she turns you on, she shouldn't have such a zero in the family closet. Makes you wonder if she doesn't have some of the same boredom genes somewhere. And where would *that* leave your taste?"

"That's pretty good, Chet."

"Fuckin' A."

He seemed to have invited the question I had already decided at least five times I wasn't going to ask him. "Try this one, then. Suppose Iler isn't all that boring. Suppose teaching English wasn't the only thing he was busy doing over here?"

He nodded far too reasonably. "The thought occurred."

The little stab in my esophagus was some of the restaurant wine demanding air. "What thought? Occurred to who?"

He shrugged. "We looked him up, of course. Has a lot of blanks where you don't usually find them. I mean, nobody should be *that* blank. He's an American, right? We spend a lot of tax money making every one of our boys and girls the most fascinating people on the globe."

"So you don't believe he could have just been teaching English?"

"If you're asking would I like to believe it, no. If you're asking can I help you keep that gleam in your eye going, no to that, too."

"You looked him up yourself?"

"King. I just saw the printout. Guy went through a lot of turnstiles and customs booths but didn't seem to do squat once he was admitted. But you're getting off the point. You just don't like boring John Iler being the brother of this chick you're horny about."

That much I—and the resettled wine in my esophagus—had an answer for. "Horseshit. Every Babbitt has a brother or sister out there who's creating a symphony or burning down the cornfields for Christ."

"'Burning down the cornfields for Christ?' What the hell's that?"

"A way of saying. Energy. Creativity. Dynamic dynamo."

"Why would Christ want anybody's cornfield burned down? To starve the planter and his family? That's supposed to be imaginative?"

"You're missing my point here, Winans."

And he didn't care; he had wild eyes only for the palazzo apartment lights across the Tiber. "Give *me* a choice between burning down a cornfield for Christ and starving people or being the biggest bore in the world like John Iler, I'll take the Iler option, if you don't mind."

"What I'm saying is I don't worry about Barbara from the point of view of what her brother might have been."

He snickered; not all that maturely but snickered anyway. And I wished I could see the same King printout he had seen.

| 21 |

THE NIGHTCLUB WAS across the street from the Tiber, but it could have been in any rural mall. Blue lights outlined a heavy orange door, a din of heavy metal rushed up from the staircase just inside the entrance. Downstairs, a glaringly lighted dance floor was raised above a broken field of divans and knee-high tables with candles. Half the people shaking on the floor looked like married couples trying not to think about what their babysitter was up to at home.

"It's not . . ."

"I know, Chet. It's not the Palladium."

"I thought that closed a long time ago."

I fell deeply into one of the couches, giving myself one scotch before calling for a cab and going back to the hotel. That suddenly seemed like a very clear direction—back to the hotel, back to the airport, back to New York, back to the apartment to see how far along Annie had gotten with packing up my stuff. Too bad I looked in another direction and saw Nino Borgato. He was slumped down on a divan against a wall, his hands folded across his stomach, gazing up at the low mirrored ceiling, while a spidery brunette in a blue minidress and her shoes off whispered something in his ear. The woman had never been a pregnant blonde working behind the counter of a Trastevere coffee house.

Winans couldn't have been prouder if he had arranged it personally. If he hadn't already blown King's authorized expenses for the evening back at the restaurant, he might have sent champagne over to Borgato and his lady friend. Peeking at Nino's contemplation of the ceiling mirror, though, I got the impression Nullo Borgato's son would have preferred powder to any liquid. He looked absolutely numb to how the woman was playing with a curl above his ear, and the tequila-looking thing on the table in front of him had been barely touched.

"He has a record," Winans said casually.

"What?"

He was suddenly all shrugs. "He did a year in Denmark for trying to bring drugs into the country a couple of years ago. The sentence was three years, but the old man apparently bought out the rest of it."

"Another printout of King's?"

"As a matter of fact. It's his job. When Borgato's name came up in the body mix-up, who knew if it was really just a shipping mistake? Some of these drug guys can get very imaginative . . . Hey, it's not like we put a full-court press on it! Routine procedures. Here's the name, press the key, see what the computer tells you. There was nothing at all against the old man, just the son."

Which, of course, left two possibilities: Either computerized records still weren't where Big Brother wanted them to be or Nino had been spinning creative tales about his father's days as a boxer, knee-breaker, and habitual guest of the police. I really didn't like the second option. "Anything else you guys have left out?"

Winans was offended. "What's the son got to do with anything? He was a small-time pusher who got caught in Copenhagen and now he runs a coffee house. And what does either one of them have to do with Iler?"

So Socrates wasn't the only one able to ask unanswerable questions. My scotch went down over my wine like glucose while I tried to relive the sense of reward I had felt when Minton had first told me about the assignment. Was I missing something or did I just want to entertain myself thinking I was?

"*L'americano!*"

One advantage of coke is only your eyes stagger; the rest of you is able to stand straight and look perfectly sober before some happy discovery.

"How's it going, Nino?"

"*Benissimo, benissimo. Cosa bevi?*"

"Nothing. I have one."

He snapped his fingers to a passing waiter for two more scotches anyway, then dropped down heavily next to me. The brunette was watching him suspiciously from their wall table.

"Who's your American friend?"

Winans extended his hand for a shake, but Nino had already lost interest in him. "They came around tonight saying they were going to dig up the grave tomorrow morning. I told them no, thank you. They said I had no choice. Why, *americano*? Why can't they leave him alone?"

"It's not your father there, Nino. It's somebody else."

"This way you can bury your father properly," Winans got in.

"We *did* bury him! Who the fuck are you to say we didn't? I'm supposed to call my mother and tell her to come down to Rome again for another funeral?"

"So leave things the way they are," Winans shrugged. "They'll just put your father where everybody thinks he's been anyway, and nobody will know the difference."

Borgato looked at me with a who-is-this-shit-next-to-you appeal, but then lapsed into silence, staring at some line that seemed to extend from his developing stomach out to the carpet under the table. Over against the wall, at the end of the line, the brunette was being very meticulous about lighting a long, thin cigarette and exhaling her first puff at the ceiling. I smelled a tantrum in the offing.

"She thinks she's a singer," Nino said, somewhere between snideness and wondrous fact.

"An opera singer?"

"*Dio santo, no!*"

Her name was Flavia, she wanted to sing like Madonna, and that was all I wanted to know about her. As long as I had to stay to drink his scotch, I wanted to hear instead about his father's opera singer. Nino was amused his teaser at the coffee house had been so effective, but I wanted to hear something more colorful than Johnny Iler's travails with the *Herald Tribune* crossword puzzle. And Winans listened as though memorizing key words for another file search in the morning.

The opera singer, Vivian Gertz, had been a double step in Nullo Borgato's climb to remake himself. More than his wife (Nino's mother) had ever understood, Nullo had begun spending weekends in art galleries, museums, and symphony halls. One opening had led to another, and his circle of acquaintances had grown steadily, reducing to a smaller and smaller dot his days with boxing gloves and metal pipes (if they had ever existed at all, of course). And if there had been a constant theme to his aesthetic bent, it had been an appreciation for all things American— American painters, American actors, American musicians. Nobody had been able to break his enthusiasm for exhibitions and performances he had spoken about as though they had been his personal productions.

"The snobs were always laughing behind his back, thought he was naive," Nino said, appropriating for himself the second scotch and ignoring Winans. "He didn't care. The opera singer was an American, she was an *ar-tiste*, and she was his special project."

"Was she any good?"

"What do I know? Papa said she was the greatest voice in Europe, all she needed was some smart impresario to help her. All I ever heard her do was shriek. I called her when Papa died, and she sounded like she was afraid I wanted some money from her for the funeral. Took forever to get an 'I'm sorry' out of her. *Una putana*."

"Why did she and your father break up?"

Even Winans looked at me oddly for that one. I was about to tell both of them I was conducting a survey on the reasons for marriage breakups when Flavia interrupted—with the accuracy of Pedro Martinez.

The next few seconds seemed to take forever. A white missile cut the distance between our table and Flavia's. Somebody shouted from the divan behind ours. Borgato got what turned out to be a plastic white ashtray in the back of the neck. He turned around too slowly to see Flavia following up with the tequila he had left behind. He barely evaded getting the glass in his face, moving just in time so that it glanced off his shoulder. Flavia let go with a torrent that reduced the rock to muzak.

Borgato let his own glass go with a weak right hand, hitting only the table in front of her. Two bouncers in matching blue jackets rushed at us from the doorway, and a third, older man in the same blue arrived from the back.

Then *my* mistakes started. I grabbed Nino from the back and pinned him down on our sofa. All three of the bouncers saw that and made the same decision to go after Flavia as the threat that was still loose. One of them wrapped his big arm around her chest, preventing her from following up on an intended charge at Nino, and that should have been enough. But then the second one from the door reached down into the dark floor and grabbed her ankles and lifted her up, clearly bent on moving her out as an unnecessary piece of furniture.

"Hey, you don't have to do that!"

Count the ways. Maybe they *did* have to move unsubtly against somebody flinging ashtrays and glasses. Maybe I should have shouted in Italian instead of English so the rest of the club wouldn't have zeroed in on our divan as the evening's unexpected entertainment. And maybe when I saw the oldest bouncer, who wasn't needed for Flavia, charge at us, I should have made some kind of international sign for fins. What I actually did do was give Nino another shove into the corner of the divan to make sure he stayed out of the action, then stand up in front of the oncoming bouncer. It was a truly noble moment: I was going to protect this guy I didn't particularly like from the forces of nightclub thuggery in surroundings I could have done without in the first place. The only trouble with so much altruism was that the bouncer had been heading for me, not Borgato, to begin with.

The last time I had seen the intense malice in the old guy's eyes had been after a fender bender on Fifth Avenue and 43rd Street. Just like the raving lunatic in New York should not have been allowed out on the street without a leash, the gray-haired bouncer who dropped both his hands on my chest with a painful thud should not have been allowed near people. Vanity says it was my astonishment at the comparison that gave him even the seconds he had to start yanking me over our table, not at all concerned if he got me to the door on my feet or along the floor.

Granted he was broader in the shoulders and had apparently dealt with my ilk before, but I still had him by inches, not only in height but also around the wrists and forearms. Even as I began prying his hands off me, I was growing as furious with the seconds he had dominated as with him.

I got in one-and-a-half pops. The first one was as good a shot as I had given anybody since Robert Pagliaroni in fifth grade: a full palm to the bouncer's jaw, sending him back over the divan on the other side of our table. The half was a punchy slap off Winans' left cheek as he made a grab to discourage me from going after the bouncer. To Chet's credit, he recoiled once, but then just covered his cheek and gaped at me as though I owed him a one-liner to make the whole experience worthwhile. I managed to say I was sorry, and I think he was disappointed.

What could have happened next didn't, and because of the unlikeliest party—Nino. Instead of the dozens more bouncers in blue I envisioned streaming out toward me from around the maze of divans, there was Borgato suddenly stumbling over his feet, clambering up to the table, and letting loose with a commanding "*E finito! E finito!*" That was enough to freeze everybody, even the bouncers who were holding the squirming Flavia like firemen dealing with an unruly net under a jumper. And then it was apologies left and right—to the club, to the other patrons, to the right of people to enjoy themselves without being bothered by ruffians— all of them delivered with a raspy, strenuous sincerity. I knew he had carried the moment when the older bouncer regained his feet, threw me a snarl, but then started beating at his knees and refitting his shoulders under his jacket. Five minutes later, Winans and I were outside watching Nino and Flavia going at it at her car some yards away. They were down to hissing at one another.

"In case you didn't notice," Chet said, "we got out without paying for our drinks."

No, I hadn't noticed, but that seemed fit only for the bottom of the list of things I hadn't. At the top? Maybe that buildup a little too easily to my eagerness to take on the bouncer. Who else had I wanted to imagine inside his blue suit? I stopped counting after Charles King, Annie, Joe McAteer, and all the forces of fascism in Singapore and Sierra Leone.

Nino insisted Flavia drive me back to the hotel, which also meant driving Winans back to his car. Flavia didn't pretend to be a good sport about it—slamming herself into the driver's seat and turning the ignition while her three passengers were still opening doors to get in. All the way to Winans' car, Nino kept up a murmuring monologue with her; it didn't do much to ease the scowl she kept on me from the rearview mirror, but it made her hold off from veering the car over the Tiber wall and drowning all of us.

When Flavia did speak, Nino wished she hadn't. We had already left the sobered up Winans at his car and were in front of my hotel. Nino was out in the street with me, adding another apology to the oration he had delivered from the nightclub table, but with more of his typical indolence, sounding very much like somebody leading up to something.

"*Mandero le foto qui*?" Flavia called from her window.

"*Ci penso io, ci penso io*," he snapped back at her, but not fast enough to stem a reddening awkwardness. He gave it a few more paces away from the car before mentioning the photographs I would be receiving.

"And what am I supposed to do with them?"

"You know," he said, as though my role in his lie to her had been part of some prearranged plan. "You like them, you give them to somebody in America who wants to hear her sing. You don't like them; you throw them in the garbage before you leave."

What could I say? His nerve was beyond measure? I didn't know a damn thing about Italian singers and even if I did, I didn't know anybody in the States who would be interested? I could throw her glossies in the wastepaper basket in my room and she would never be the wiser, just as long as he could keep getting laid? What I did, of course, was try to be helpful. "If she's a singer, she needs demos, not pictures."

"Yeah, yeah, that's what I keep telling her. But the only thing she's got is when she was with a group a few years ago. CDs cost money."

"So have a concert at the coffee house and record it."

He should have pointed out I was being a wiseass for suggesting Flavia and his wife under the same roof; instead, he looked taken with the idea. "I got to think about that," he said, one budding entrepreneur to another. "But see what you can do too, okay? And if you want to hear any more about Papa's opera singer before you leave, drop by. *Ciao.*"

It was a brushoff, a fuck-you, a thank-you, and an invitation all in one. It was galling, but, watching him hurry back to the car, I also admired the open sleaziness of it all.

And wondered if he had learned it from his father.

| 22 |

SO HERE WAS Happy walking back into his room and thinking about what a marvelously technicolor world we live in, about all the appetizing printouts in Charles King's desk drawer, and about taking a couple of aspirin to head off the morning blues. That's how the day should have ended, anyway. But the phone in my room had different ideas. "I was looking out the window, saw your friends dropping you off," Barbara said.

"There are pictures to like and pictures not to like."

"Excuse me?"

She had been direct about calling, I thought, so I had to reciprocate. "The pictures I like are you standing at the window wondering where the hell I am because you missed me. The pictures I don't like are you just wanting to explain something about your dinner tonight."

"Do I owe you an explanation?"

"For the dinner, no. For the coyness about maybe eating with me when you knew all along you wouldn't be? Maybe."

"But neither one of us really want to talk about that."

"Stupid me. That's right."

Vision: When you don't know what you're talking about, when every word seems to lead you further down some obscure trail toward the darkest of woods, you know *exactly* what you're talking about, you just don't want to be reminded of it. But I couldn't even stay on that track with her. "How far out in front?" I asked for both of us.

"What?"

"The words we're putting ahead of ourselves to see if we can catch up. I've caught up. What're you doing? What do you want to do? Do you want me to be part of it?"

The answer was her whispery laugh, not a trace of embarrassment in it. "I guess I do, or I wouldn't have called. We could meet at the bar if it's still open."

"We've been there. And in the lobby and in the elevator."

"Then I guess you better come up here."

I thought manly things going up the fire stairs. How much had my deodorant worn off? How much too much had I drunk? Had the night-club scotch worked as mouthwash for the restaurant wine? And what was the deal on adultery? If you were already being kicked out of your apartment (and no matter what Annie said, it was *never* too late for aggressors and victims), did going to bed with somebody else fit the term? It felt really good reaching the fourth floor and slamming the heavy, barred door on all those existential matters.

Only her bed-table lamp was on, giving the room more wall shadows than light. What I had accepted as aerosol deodorant in my room smelled like just a smothered layer of hotel mustiness under the scents from the dresses on the open closet hooks and the small collection of vials and bottles on the bureau. "Charlotte was a nice woman," Barbara said, when I asked about the six-pack of mineral water and bags of popcorn also on the bureau. "As soon as I mentioned my room didn't have one of those little refrigerators, she insisted on giving me a CARE package. You're too late for the chocolates."

"Winans makes Mrs. King sound like a pain in the ass."

"Not at all. I felt a little sorry for her."

"Being married to King?"

She curled her legs up under her on the plastic lounger next to the window and nodded. She had broken her pact with solids again: jeans and a threadbare gray sweater that revealed her shoulder bones. "She's really the hostess-wife. All these married couples from the embassy who wait for Charles to say something because he outranks them. He outranks her, too."

"I don't think I want to hear about it."

I had never seen a moue face before; pouty and sulky faces, but never quite the moue she turned on me. "I was about to tell you how I gave her oxygen for a few hours. Talking about her daughter and Wise Owlie and Dinky Dog."

"Now I know I don't want to hear about it."

"Sharon, that's the daughter, was having trouble at the International School when they first moved here. She didn't like being away from her friends in Madrid, their last posting . . ."

"Barbara?"

". . . Fortunately for all concerned, the kindergarten had some of my books, and Charlotte had already read them to Sharon in Spain. The way Charlotte put it, Dinky Dog and Zelda the Zebra became stabilizing influences for the girl. Gave her a sense of continuity, a security."

"That's nice."

More moue: "I thought so. It's nice to know you can be important to people for reasons that never occur to you."

"If I made love to you right now, would it be just to you or to Dinky and all the gang?"

She glanced at the knee folded under her as though needing its permission to answer. "Depends. If you tickle me, it'll make me think of Giggly Goose."

"Is that good?"

"Again, depends. On when."

"Much later."

She nodded. "After the serious parts."

I kissed her just as a motor scooter turned off from the Via Veneto and went speeding down the street. It sounded bleaty and bronchial at the same time. I had never thought of that combination before and couldn't imagine what kind of an animal it would have made for transferred to a pasture or a jungle. Whatever it was, I wanted to be it.

| 23 |

"I WAS ABOUT to throw water on you."

There was something like daylight outside the window, morning plus a drizzly rain. She was sitting up against the headboard. She had put the gray sweater back on, but her panties were the yellow legal pad she was standing against her raised thighs. Not only was the page in front of her half-filled, but other pages heavy with her broad hand had been turned over the top of her knees. "You look halfway through *War and Peace*."

She wrote another sentence more urgent than Lover Returns to Consciousness. "I've been up an hour. You looked content."

"Am I?"

She smiled, as much at what her pen was writing as at me. "You should be."

"That was yesterday."

In another life, she must have been a second baseman turning a double play. She dipped down under my tug, all soft and flexible and soap-smelling, but not yielding a jot from her pen. "If you were a squirrel, what would your name be?"

"Squiggly."

Call it another Moment of Greatness, as back at King's office. She looked at me in such dismay I didn't know why all the splashy morning noises below the window also didn't fall silent in amazement at having me among them. "That's right!"

"It's not really much of a reach . . ."

Ba-dum! Down went the pad on the sheet, down went the pen on the pad, down went her legs. "Obvious, you mean?"

So make it worse. "Isn't that good for children's stories?"

"There's a difference between obvious and accessible."

"So call him Squishy."

"Squishy's a squid."

"Then Squirrely."

"That *is* obvious."

"Okay. So Squiggly it is."

"On second thought that sounds like a worm."

"No, that would be . . ." Oh, shut up.

She folded her arms over her small breasts and scanned the bureau mirror at the foot of the bed for something. "You don't think this is serious, do you?"

"Of course it is. It's what you do."

"*I* know it's serious. I'm asking if you think it is."

Vision: When you're itching for a fight, squirrels can be as handy as anything else. So I didn't think I was hazarding too much by broadening the front. "This all has something to do with Alicia yesterday, doesn't it? All those trolls and things on her walls."

She lifted her right foot with painstaking slowness up from the sheet; it might have been an exercise; it might have just been to put her foot between her face and the mirror. "Johnny never grew up," she said, trying to sound nonchalant. "She was old enough to be his mother."

"His choice."

It was an exercise, but not a physical one; by concentrating on raising her foot centimeter by centimeter, she could make the strain sound like it belonged to something besides Alicia Silvestri. "Children don't have choices," she said, trying to look diverted by her arch. "They have whims, impulses, fears. In case you haven't noticed, I know something about it. It's made me a living."

"It seems to have gotten Johnny an apartment, too."

"That supposed to provoke me?"

"He couldn't have afforded that place on a teacher's salary."

She looked satisfied with the pulsating around her knee. "No, he couldn't," she conceded. "So maybe your two blackbirds were right. Maybe he *was* making money on the side from something else."

"You mean, believe that or believe he was being kept by Alicia?"

She had more moues than one: This one was a slide over to amusement that didn't see anything particularly funny. "Yes. Do you mind?"

The telephone stopped me from having to answer. "How are you this morning, Charles? I want to thank you again for . . ." She sat up so fast she scrunched her legal pad and all the squirrels on it. "But what does that mean, Charles?"

King kept talking, she kept narrowing her eyes, and somebody kept blowing a horn down in the street. When it all finally ended, she was still reluctant to let go of the dead receiver. "It wasn't Borgato in the casket," she announced, looking at me to put color back in her face. "It was somebody named Borla."

It was my fault, I thought. I hadn't believed Fred Cleary in the opening scene, so now the extraterrestrials were showing me how they always thrived and multiplied on idiot skepticism.

| 24 |

DEPENDING ON YOUR point of view, it was screwup on top of screwup or the straightening out of two screwups. The first buffoonery had been shipping somebody besides Johnny Iler to New York. The second one had been identifying the body in that casket as Nullo Borgato. Both of those follies had been signed off on by Daniela Gallo, a hospital mortuary director who had clearly done Italy a favor by not specializing in brain surgery. But then, as the papers were being prepared at the mortuary in Gallo's absence for authorizing the reopening of the Borgato grave, some underling (one of those *idioti*) had stumbled across a mess with the fingerprints file and had taken it upon himself to do a second matching with the transatlantic file. It was this Gallo assistant who had started the phone calls.

Of course, whether it was screwup-atop-screwup-atop-screwup or the straightening out of two screwups, that remained only half the problem. Another 40 percent of it was that nobody could find records anywhere of the most logical resting place for Iler—Lamberto Borla's grave. As Cleary had already informed me, there wasn't a single document establishing that Borla's body had been released by the hospital. And the other 10 percent? Now that there was no more solid evidence that Nullo Borgato had been one of the mishandled corpses, son Nino was back to objecting to any tampering with his father's grave, and this time with the backing of an attorney.

But at least as far as King and an Interior Ministry inspector named Gozzi were concerned, Nino posed no great problem. Gozzi, a heavyset 50-year-old whose jet-black cowlick was supposed to make him look 15 years younger and who was totally indifferent to the signs in King's office asking visitors not to smoke, had an infinite supply of reassuring smiles for Barbara. "Once this becomes a criminal investigation, Signorina, the Borgato family can hire every lawyer in Europe, but we will still have the right to open the grave. The question is, do we want to go on the assumption it is a criminal inquiry and obtain that authorization?"

Stiff in her chair at King's conference table, Barbara waited for more, but Gozzi just took another puff. "You're asking *me*?"

King gave off another of the nervous coughs he had been contributing since meeting us at the reception desk and leading us back to his office. "What the inspector means, Barbara, is there may be quieter ways of dealing with this than an all-out investigation."

"At least until you find out everybody in the country is buried in the wrong place."

King looked nipped, but Gozzi laughed heartily. "The Signorina may have a point."

"When do negligence and incompetence become criminal?"

Gozzi considered my question reasonable. "The problem precisely. Does this melancholy confusion merit more than an official letter to Dottoressa Gallo's superiors or do we pursue the line that two, maybe three, families have been deprived of their rights?"

Gozzi's friendliness toward me had been thicker than his cigarette smoke from the moment we had shaken hands. I had also sensed abnormally good behavior from King, as though the two of them had agreed it wasn't the moment to alienate the forces of New York tabloids. At least this time, I was right, if for the wrong reasons.

"Charles says you might be helpful here, Signore. I gather you know the Borgato son. Would it be too much for you to explain the situation to him in an informal way? Mind you, we don't have much optimism about finding Signorina Iler's brother in the Borgato grave at this point, but it remains a minimal possibility and it would be good to resolve at least that part of the problem as quickly as we can."

I absorbed it in pieces and fragments. Evidently, Chet Winans had been doing more reporting than I had lately. Barbara stared at me as though I shouldn't even have been hesitating to volunteer my services. King might have been cursing himself for having let me in his office the first time, let alone the second time. And then there was the Dottoressa. "Nobody seems eager to take on this Gallo woman. She just runs one mortuary in one hospital, doesn't she?"

Gozzi went up another level in his benevolent smiles. "As these positions go, it's an especially visible one. Skills are important, of course, but don't forget we're also in Rome."

"The folklore argument."

His smile was slightly less benevolent. "In a day or two, you'll be back in America," he said, squashing out his cigarette or me in the ashtray, "but I'll still be here within reach of too many telephones. Nothing tragic, but tiring. You must have the same problem when you write about somebody who objects to being written about."

No, Minton took those calls, I thought about saying—except he wouldn't be taking them much longer if I didn't file something that evening. But why accent the negative? Despite Barbara's drilling look for reminding me how personal my priorities should have been, hadn't I also just been handed a very professional bargaining chip? "I'll talk to Nino in exchange for everything you have on this Borla and how his release records seem to have just vanished."

"We don't know the answer to that yet."

"But you can be working on it while I talk to Nino, right?"

Gozzi didn't think that was much of a concession. "When we discover something, you'll be the first member of the media to know."

"Even if what you discover brings you back on a collision course with Gallo and those phone calls?"

Official people can make the mistake of answering smarmy questions, but they rarely make the mistake of answering speculatively smarmy ones. Gozzi lighted another cigarette; he had said all he was going to say for the moment.

| 25 |

ONCE OUT OF the embassy, Barbara insisted on going to the coffee house with me. As she put it while waving down a taxi for both of us: "Maybe I can make him understand this isn't about a lot of clever favors going back and forth, but about finding my brother."

She might have been overrating Nino Borgato's receptivity, but she was right in a more important way. I didn't need Minton to remind me that reporters shouldn't become actors in their own stories, and I shouldn't have needed anybody to remind me the Johnny Iler Story was about her, not me. So why *did* I need the reminder as I piled into the cab after her?

Nino wasn't at the coffee house, but the rest of his family was. Two boys below school age were running in and out of the unoccupied tables scaring each other with rubber lizards, while the pregnant wife was being testy with a repairman working on the coffee machine. The TV set behind the bar was showing an old black-and-white movie with Anna Magnani fitted out as a noblewoman. The total lack of customers in the place and the sun trying to break through the slate morning made Anna look even more overdressed.

"No coffee," Borgato's wife waved before we had stepped completely inside. "No machine."

"We came to see Nino, Signora."

"No Nino," she waved again, this time making it sound like "*No Nino for you—ever, goodbye, leave me in peace.*"

"Do you know when he'll be in?"

She was irked I got as far as the bar, then altogether defeated at the sight of Barbara going directly to a table, sitting down, and sticking out her tongue at the boys who had stopped their scampering around to gape at her. "I don't know," she said less forcefully. "Come later."

"It's very important, Signora. It's about his father."

She had heard enough about my first visit not to be surprised. "His father is dead. And you want to go to the cemetery? Nino says no. That is all I know."

The repairman made the mistake of using a clean cup under the spout he was testing, so she had to redirect her impatience with me for a moment. "Ask for some tea," Barbara called. "There's water, and I can see the teabags from here."

It was how the Marx Brothers, the Doobie Brothers, and all the other great teams had succeeded: Each one had brought a special quality to the mix. Barbara contributed the comely lady who was going to be served at all costs. Signora Borgato supplied the irritation of somebody outmaneuvered. And I was on hand as the interpreter for Barbara's questions about how far along the Signora was on her third child, what the boys' names were, and which of them was the bigger handful. And as it had with the Marxes and the Doobies, it worked. Ten minutes later, Signora Borgato was simply Camilla, she was seated with us over tea, and she was doing her best to ignore the running boys and train her annoyance on the fiddling repairman.

"Every time he comes, he says the machine is old and should be replaced. Then he does something to make sure it gets older."

There were black roots to Camilla Borgato's blonde hair and there was still a hint of softness in her eyes, but one thing seemed as remote in her past as the other. Had there actually been a specific day when she had seen some blonde movie star, been overwhelmed with envy, and run home to her bathroom with bottles of dye? Had there actually been a time when she had seen only the Nino she wanted to see and had imagined their children only as more of them together? There had to have been, but the weariness slumping her shoulders down toward her heavy belly, a black print dress thrown over everything, seemed to make that irrelevant. Flavia and the odd snort in Tiber nightclubs seemed like the least of it.

"All this business is making Nino nervous," she said, probing at her lemon piece with her spoon. "He is always nervous when it has to do with Nullo. We say close your debts with the dead, but between Nino and his father . . ."

She left the thought hanging, put down her spoon, and sipped her tea. I remembered what Winans had said about Nullo paying off Nino's prison sentence in Denmark with his pension money and wondered where she had been during all that.

"It would just eliminate one possibility," Barbara said to Camilla's nods. "God knows I don't want your father-in-law's grave disturbed. If there were any other way, I wouldn't bother you. But he's my brother . . ."

I interpreted for the record, but Camilla hadn't needed the words. I was still yammering on when she reached across the table to put her hand over Barbara's. There couldn't have been more than a year or two between them, but Barbara's long, pale fingers looked childishly slight under the broad, spotted hold. "Sometimes Nino's head . . . *si gira*," she said. "We'll get a lawyer and defend the Borgato name from all these *fascisti* of the state that want to cheat him! We'll sue them and make a lot of money! Tomorrow is always going to be a miracle! Look around you. This *americanata* was his idea. All these people in America had places like this, so this was the easy way to make money. It's insanity, I tell him. America is America, Rome is Rome. If you want to open a bar, we'll try to get a bar. But not something like this where people just sit around and order nothing all day. How can he expect to succeed this way?"

The oddity had been staring me in the face since my first visit, but only Camilla's exasperation let me see it. "You say this place was Nino's idea. But it goes back to his father's time. The 1950s, 1960s."

She looked almost merry as she turned back to scold one of the kids who had found great fun in pulling magazines off the wall rack and splattering them on the floor. "Everything for Nullo was America," she said, accepting the fake look of regret the boy gave her. "You went to the cinema; you went to see the Americans. You didn't speak English; you weren't a man. When Nino . . . he had some trouble out of the country one time, and when he came back, Nullo told him to find a new start, be responsible for his family. He filled his head with all these stories of the people with the beards and berets."

"Beatniks?"

"Them!"

"That was Nullo's idea of being responsible?"

"Nino and I laughed, too. They were when Nullo had been young. So many years ago. And all they ever seemed to do was sit around playing bongo drums and smoking marijuana. But then after we laughed at all the foolishness, Nino would suddenly become cross, accuse me of mocking his father when Nullo only wanted to help us. And then he would go out and buy these books about these beatniks. Nullo would give him others. So one day we end up with this place."

"Did Nullo come often?"

"*Boh*! Once or twice. He and Nino were always fighting. About each other. About Nino's mother. About the opera singer."

"If we could check the grave today or tomorrow," Barbara put in firmly, "we could avoid a lot of problems. The police are threatening to make this a criminal investigation."

I had no choice but to translate, once again postponing the fat lady's final aria. The word *police* sent a red line up the side of Camilla's face, and she stared all the harder to distract my attention from it. "These are things you have to tell Nino."

"But you could help, Camilla. All Barbara wants to do is put this behind her. You could get Nino to help."

"That would be . . ."

Novel? Nothing to count on? Fill in the space. She didn't. Instead, she just picked up her spoon and squeezed some more brown juice out of her teabag. "Tell the Signorina," she said, eyes fixed on her saucer, "I will talk to Nino when he comes in and he will call her later. Tell her I feel sorry for the trouble she is having, that nobody should be put through this. Tell her Nino will be happy to help, he just hasn't been thinking clearly lately. He's like his father that way. Along comes a singer and he doesn't think about other people's feelings."

Obviously, Flavia wasn't going to be making her demo at the coffee house.

| 26 |

I COULD HAVE stayed with Barbara at the hotel waiting for Nino to call or I could have dropped around to Iler's school to get some quotes for filing my first piece with Minton. Credit one of my better rationalizations for expanding the field beyond those choices. If I began filing that day, wouldn't I have been inviting both the other New York papers and the Italian dailies to camp out on the story? At the risk of frazzling Minton's patience, wouldn't it have been better to tie up everything before opening fire? At the very least, I should have had official confirmation Borgato was safely interred under his own headstone, right?

I couldn't have agreed with myself more. So, instead of dealing with Barbara or Johnny or any other member of the Iler family, I followed Camilla's directions to the postal substation where Nullo Borgato had apparently spent a good part of his life. Borgato had pulled ahead of Iler again in the stakes for interesting me? I didn't card the races; I just ran them. Besides, I took it as an extremely significant omen that the substation was tucked into a back street off the Corso Vittorio, near the Basilica of Andrea della Valle: I had once attended a poetry reading by Gregory Corso with a girl named Andrea Stewart. How ominous does an omen have to be?

As for what I was looking for, I decided to let it tell me as soon as I found it. *It* turned out to be Pietro Milano.

He was a beet-faced man well into his 60s with a head of white hair that would have been the envy of any wig maker. His hair wasn't just full, it had waves on top of waves, none of them betraying imminent scalp. He was also somebody who saw no reason for speaking when he could shout. Even as I was asking the clerk behind the counter to direct me to anyone who had worked with Borgato, Milano boomed out from a workspace I couldn't see that he was the man I was looking for. A moment later, he appeared from around a divider wall, took me in with maliciously merry eyes, and waved me down to the far end of the counter. Whatever the clerk mumbled to him as we headed for the corner brought a sardonic fuck-you.

"Nullo Borgato, Nullo Borgato," he said, savoring the name with a grin. "I miss having him around here. When things went bad, you could always count on him to make them worse. What do you care about him?"

I stammered through a response near enough to the truth to delight him even more. And then he said the same thing Nino had said: "He lived in chaos, so why shouldn't he die that way?"

"That's what his son said."

The red face was immediately darker. "That *farabutto*! There's an expert you should be listening to!"

Peddling a little piece of Nino didn't seem altogether unethical. "I know about what happened in Denmark."

He was impressed with me, but not all that much. It dawned on me that all the stories—from Nino and then Camilla—had been gratis, I hadn't had to ask anything, even suggest I was interested in hearing any of them. Milano, on the other hand, had a turnstile between us.

"You're interested in him because you're a reporter? You want to interview me for some American paper?"

"Not exactly."

"Then why?"

His challenge threw me back on the only thought I had. "Because Borgato sounds interesting. A lot more interesting than anything else around me right now."

"Just because he's dead? Because his body may not be where it's supposed to be?"

A woman came out from the back with a big canvas sack and looked over at the two of us curiously. I wanted her to open the sack and drop Milano into it. But she walked over to the clerk with her problem, instead. "It's more than that . . ."

"More than that! Good! So where you taking me for lunch?"

"I didn't know I was taking you anywhere."

"With the expense account they give you in America? You don't expect me to pay, I hope."

| 27 |

MILANO LIKED HIS gags, even if one came at the expense of another. Whatever visions he might have truly entertained of a lavish meal paid for by the New York press, he decided there was more immediate fun to be had by going directly across the street from the post office to a place that was half cafeteria and half delicatessen. As we stood in front of the high glass counter pointing the counterman to the *suppli* and sandwiches we wanted, he made sure I didn't miss the point of his choice. "Like some place in New York, yes? You don't sit down and get served like civilized people. You point out the day-old food, they throw it on paper plates, then you carry it yourself while you look for a table. Feel at home?"

"No, I see forks. We're used to eating with our hands."

"Italian inefficiency. We never get it quite right."

I decided Milano was an onion. The top layer—the one where his boorishness might have gotten him a smack in the mouth—was the easiest to strip off. The next layer—where he wanted you to see the irony beneath his boorishness—came off pretty easily, too. The third layer—where he did feel aggrieved about some of the things he was spouting about—sent out ticklish fumes. The fourth layer—where he seemed to wonder why anyone would care what irritated him, genuinely or not—was a little too much meal for me after 20 minutes of knowing him and maybe always would be. And who needed to get down to a fifth layer and start tearing?

"I was in Nullo's neighborhood a few days before he died," he said, as we set our trays on a spindly table in the crowded, chilly back of the cafeteria. "The *bravo* Ninetto opened the door and told me his father was in the hospital with pneumonia. I asked him if I could come in and phone a mutual friend of ours around the corner, figuring the two of us could visit Nullo in the hospital. Nino acted like I wanted the apartment. Finally, he lets me in to use the phone, but I had to be quick, he said, because he was expecting an urgent 'business' call. This with the glitter hanging off his nose! 'Your father's in the hospital and sounds like he's in bad condition,' I said to him. 'So why aren't you up there with him instead of acting like the rat who's going to play with the cat gone?' And he gives me some more of his sniffles and says, 'Milano, my father may be impressed by you because you talk louder than he does, but I'm not. Mind your goddamn business.'" He shrugged. "He was right, of course. I wasn't even a close friend of Nullo's. We worked together, that was all."

Call it word association. Call it a dim mind. But it was only when I reached down for my second *suppli* and remembered Milano's crack at the counter about the paper plates that a pretty elementary question occurred to me. "What about the funeral? The casket?"

"What about it? We all met at the hospital where they released the casket, and we had a procession out to Campo Verano. Borgato wasn't a religious man. At least the son and the ex-wife got that right."

"But the casket with Lamberto Borla had Borgato's name on it. So what about the nameplate on the casket you took out to the cemetery?"

"It must have said Borgato, too. I didn't notice."

"But there *was* a nameplate."

"I don't know. It was covered by flowers."

"But the engraver, whoever the hospital gets to do these things, he wouldn't have made two nameplates with the same name."

"*Ow*, what do I know? It isn't the hospital that commissions these things, anyway. It's the families."

The simplest answer, of course, was that there had been no plate on the casket Milano had accompanied to the cemetery, that the only one with Borgato's name had been on Borla's coffin, and that nobody had ordered one for Borla. But even that solution still left a missing nameplate for Iler.

"What? Spit it out, *americano*."

It was an absolutely ridiculous thought, worthy of Fred Cleary's conspiracies. But then again, how much more ludicrous was it than the idea that Johnny Iler had been some kind of spook? The nice thing about absurd fantasies was that they made the subsequent ones conjured up easier to swallow. "Suppose somebody could still be alive?"

Shock? Astonishment? Bafflement that the United States of America could let somebody like me travel around freely? No, Milano couldn't have been happier at the idea. There had been much to mock about America over the years: Donald Trump, George W. Bush, Bill Clinton and Monica Lewinsky, the Vietnam Follies, all the way back to George Washington's wooden teeth. But until I had come along, he had never truly seen the possibilities. "Wonderful!" he boomed to the annoyance of the couple at the tiny table next to ours. "So any second now we can expect Borgato to walk in and join us for lunch, that it? Wonderful! Nullo Borgato haunting all our lives. We don't see him, but he sees us. He sees old Milano getting up in the morning, putting his bones back where they belong, and trudging down to work. He sees old Milano walking into the magic nectar of the station—vomit a kid deposited in the place 10 years ago, cigar smells . . . "

"Okay, okay."

"But why not? You go through this elaborate charade to make everyone think you're dead and then you spend your new existence hovering over your old one. Give me a better vision of the afterlife."

"So I said something stupid. Something you've never done, I'm sure."

Finally, something like a hit. He looked down at his sandwich with a skepticism that looked close to an admission. "The fact is," he said after a moment, "Borgato had more reason than most to disappear the way you're saying . . ."

"I'm not saying . . ."

"Speculating, dreaming, needing—it's all the same, isn't it? The funny thing is, I was thinking something like that at the funeral. To see some of the people there, it was like a gathering of vultures. What do you call those birds in America? The ones in the cowboy movies?"

"Buzzards."

"Yes. There were a lot of buzzards at Nullo's funeral."

"Like who?"

"You wouldn't know them."

"I know that, Pietro. That's why I'm asking."

He was back to studying me with a twinkle in his eye. "First of all, don't call me Pietro like I'm a cathedral for the tourists. Piero or Milano. Second, what do you care?"

"I told you."

"You told me why you were interested in the dead Borgato. Now you're asking something else."

He had mercy on my dumb silence and resumed chewing his ham sandwich. "Ninetto, of course," he offered after another moment. "That's one he would be relieved to get away from. All the son ever gave him was lawyers and cops. Bankers, too, where that coffee house is concerned."

"The father paid for that?"

"How much I don't know. But he moaned to me about the loans he had to take out for Nino. That's why Princigalli was at the funeral."

"Who's that?"

"Somebody you don't know."

"Yes, I'm aware of that, too."

"Okay, okay. Years ago, Nullo helped Princigalli get a job with the printer that published the post office newsletter. He went to Princigalli for a loan for the coffee house. He might as well have gone to the Mafia. The only reason Princigalli was at the funeral was he couldn't believe Borgato was really dead, that his monthly extortion was at an end."

"So without Borgato continuing to pay off the loan, Nino's in danger of losing the place?"

"Tell me you care about that too and I'll wonder what they're putting in American beer."

"There's the wife and the kids . . ."

"Ah, yes, Camilla Lecco! Her father threw her out when she started using the family living room for Ninetto's cocaine deals. Then she stole some money to help him buy drugs in Denmark. When they arrested him, she went to Nullo and convinced him he wouldn't be much of a father or a grandfather if he let Nino rot in jail up there."

"Borgato told you this?"

"No, I got a telegram this morning. What do you think?"

"She doesn't look like she's on anything right now."

He shrugged indifferently. "So she found Jesus or the Reverend Moon or the European Community. Or maybe—can it be?—she cares about her children. What do you think, *americano?*"

We had somehow slipped down between the fourth and fifth layer of the onion. The man's anger for people, things, and all the molecules between them seemed depthless. "Is it just the people around Borgato you don't like, or do you drink a cup of acid for breakfast every morning?"

There was an odd pride in his smile. "Tuscans are realists and I invented Tuscany."

For some reason, that was enough to prompt the couple next to us to gather up their napkins and paper plates and move away. Milano threw a mock salute after them. "That's the problem with this place. You can't choose who you don't want to be next to."

We seemed safely back at the first layer of simple boorishness. "Who else was at the funeral?"

"Let's see. There was Tortola. A *ruffiano* who calls himself an art dealer. He has a hole-in-the-wall gallery on the Via Babuino, but the next painting he sells will be the first one. He's always got *affari* going on in his back room, and I think Nullo was involved in them more than he should have been. He had the same look as Princigalli at the funeral. Like he'd given Nullo something on consignment and now he couldn't get it back because Nullo had been so thoughtless to die."

Milano savored running down the list. A married Communist Party official from the old days who had depended on Borgato's apartment for his trysts. An opera company manager who had never done anything for the infamous opera singer Vivian. A sculptor. A tram conductor.

The operator of an illegal casino. An entertainment reporter for a daily newspaper. Many women—this magazine editor and that boutique owner—who thought his maladroit Latin Lover approaches flattered them in front of their husbands and boyfriends. All of them had detected a use in Nullo Borgato that he had mistaken for friendship, sympathy, or promises for a better tomorrow.

I had to fight a deepening gloom to ask him: "And what was your contribution? You say you weren't a close friend, but you sound like some encyclopedia on his life. You just drop by the apartment, but a second later you're organizing a visit to the hospital."

"So?"

"You know exactly what I'm asking. All these other people seemed to have their hypocritical uses for him. What was yours?"

For a second, he seemed to be gauging what layer of the onion I was for him. Then he decided he could live with it. "Same as yours, *americano*," he said evenly. "I lost someone I felt magnificently superior to."

He deserved his water, I thought.

| 28 |

NINO BORGATO PROVED to be as accommodating as Camilla had assured us; from my point of view, Gozzi even more so. Although Nino's permission to open the grave was relayed to the Italian cop before three o'clock, he decided to wait until after nightfall, after the cemetery had been closed, to send in the shovels. Even Minton agreed that made it premature for me to file anything right away.

"Which isn't to say you can't send something midnight your time," he quibbled.

"Same problem, Ed. You're going to want Borgato family reactions, and who the hell am I to roust them so late?"

He gave me a cigarette cough to see the error of my ways, but I stayed blind. "Since when do we care about that family's reactions?" he finally gave in. "You'll have the sister, the city government suits, and the embassy. In case you've forgotten, you're not doing this for *Il Corriere* Whatever."

I had already rehearsed for that objection. "The Italians are going to jump all over this when they hear about it, and that means AP will be right behind them. I can stay ahead of them another day or so just because I know all the players. But let's make full use of the players."

"There's one thing I can't stand in this world, Danny."

"I know. Bullshit."

"No, not bullshit. If I couldn't stand that, I wouldn't be at this desk so long. What I can't stand is not knowing what the bullshit is aimed at. It makes me feel vulnerable. Do I have to protect my balls or my back? Help me out with that one, kid."

I had prepared for that one, too, but I felt a little cheap actually having to say it. "Yesterday I told you there were three bodies involved, and you didn't believe me. Now what I'm telling you is there's a possibility—mark that word *possibility*—one of the bodies might not be so dead."

"Get outta here!"

It went smoothly after that; at least until he was about to hang up. "Did Annie get you? She called last night for the name of your hotel. You didn't give me any reason not to give it to her."

"She didn't say what she wanted?"

"Yeah, Russell Crowe. But I could only advise her to wait until she got rid of you. Talk to you."

I hung up, ticking off a dozen reasons why Annie might need to talk to me in a hurry. The most logical was she just wanted to know when I was coming home, and the rest weren't worthy even of me. I decided against calling her at work. Even in our best days, she had always sounded like an automaton speaking from her office, as though some Uriah Heap of a boss was about to deduct pennies from her salary for every minute on the phone.

Then Barbara knocked on my door. She smiled too quickly and banged her loose fists together too anxiously as she walked in. "I thought I could get some writing done," she said, going over to the window to see how my view compared to hers, "but I can't concentrate. My God, I hope a truck doesn't try to get down this street. It will plow right in here."

"You get to meet people that way."

"And who'd you get to meet today? Did you go to Johnny's school?"

Mentioning Piero Milano suddenly felt like disloyalty. "Just walked around a bit."

"You should have told me. I would have gone with you."

"You wanted to be back for Nino's call, remember."

I suppose we could have gone on like that for another hour, but we didn't. I felt as relieved as she sounded when I got over to her and touched her trembling. "It's like I have to wait for him to die all over again," she said, kicking off her tan shoes. "I don't want to be alone for that. Please rub my feet."

| 29 |

A LIGHT RAIN WAS falling when King and Winans picked us up at the hotel at 8:30. The 20-minute ride was through homogenized neighbor-hoods of medium high-rises being held up by open bars and shuttered laundromats. Winans concentrated on driving, King tried to sound opinionated about traffic lights versus zebra crossings, and Barbara stared sightlessly out her window, her body tense under her raincoat and jeans. When she coughed and took a tube of mints from her pocket, she moved the silence so obtrusively that Winans looked at her through his rearview mirror and King looked back at her in concern. Only when she wrapped her tongue around the mint and put her hands back in her pockets did the crisis end.

I thought about the last time I had gone to a cemetery—for my Aunt Allie's funeral. Crossing the Verrazzano Bridge to Staten Island that day, with only Annie and me in the single limousine hired for the occa-sion, I had felt cheated. At 66, Aunt Allie had barely qualified for her Senior Citizen discounts, and she had been the longest survivor from her generation of the strokes, cancers, and heart attacks that had wiped out my mother, father, two uncles, and another aunt in a seven-year period before I had reached 25. Couldn't at least one of them have endured to be on hand to see me accept the Pulitzer Prize?

And there had been something nastier that cold, sunny morning in Staten Island, too—something not all that unrelated to my ambivalence about which body I wanted Gozzi's people to find in the Borgato grave. Sitting next to Annie in the limo, I had wondered why, while my family had been erased from the planet, her bastard of a father looked to be around to ring the Liberty Bell for the goddamn tricentennial. Somebody somewhere should have had the power to make a trade, I remembered thinking. Maybe Joe McAteer in exchange for a parent. Tasteless, but there it was.

When we arrived at the cemetery gate, it became clear King should have made one more call before setting out. The cemetery guard and the two cops drafted for the evening hadn't been expecting any onlookers and weren't about to let any in. As King became more irate, and equally determined not to display it before Barbara, Winans leaned out his window and calmly suggested the cops check with the on-scene official in charge of the disinterment. One of the cops peered in the car at Barbara, then clomped off a few yards in his heavy boots, radioed to somebody from his motorcycle, listened, then turned and waved to a guard in the gatehouse to open up.

"It never stops," King muttered, not spelling out what *it* was.

As far away as the equivalent of three or four blocks, we could see the lights that had been set up under the cypresses and around the Borgato tomb. There were at least a dozen uniformed and plainclothes people at the site, where the coffin was already being raised by a winch. Nobody seemed too concerned about the rain, which had picked up to a heavy ribbon tempo since we had left the hotel.

Gozzi detached himself from the other spectators as Winans pulled up. "Stay in the car, you'll only get wet," he said, keeping his cigarette behind his back as he leaned down at King's window. "There's a chamber down at the end of the grounds where we will do the examination. That is Rinaldi from the hospital."

He nodded to a young, bald guy who was apparently filling in for the Dottoressa Gallo. Nobody at all seemed to be filling in for Nino Borgato.

"We sent a car to the coffee bar," Gozzi shrugged. "His wife had the papers. She didn't sound like he would be here."

Barbara's intake of breath could have been mine: Was Nino's absence it—the final omen we were about to find Johnny Iler and not his father? Iler didn't have to be *that* much of a blank slate, did he?

Rain or not, King got out of the car, telling Winans to proceed down to where the identification would take place while he conferred with Gozzi. Chet did what he was told, rolling to the far end of the cemetery as slowly as he could. Our destination was a stone bunker with an iron gate. A police car was stationed in front of the thing, and a light shone from inside.

"Odd, Borgato couldn't bother to be here," Winans said. "Suppose it's not his father?"

Barbara dug her hands into her pockets more deeply; if her tube of mints had been a gun, Winans would have been dead. "It's not going to be," I reminded him.

He looked around as though I had sent him a coded message. "Oh, Jesus, yeah," he said, a sickly smile for Barbara. "I was just talking from his point of view. You'd think he would care more."

"I don't care about his point of view, Chet."

He nodded, pretending to contemplate the wisdom, not the ice, of her reply, then turned back in his seat to study the bunker more scrupulously.

Thanks to Winans' gaffes, a minivan with the body pulled up next to us faster than I had expected. As the cemetery workers and a cop slid the coffin out of the back and hefted it inside to the bunker, I knew I didn't want to do any more waiting in the car. "They won't let us in there," Barbara said, as I opened the door.

"I just want some air. Come on. You have a raincoat."

I wished I'd had mine. But once out into the sloppy, sweet air, my corduroy jacket and sweater seemed like the first commitment I had made in ages and I knew I couldn't go back on it. My nerve was rewarded when Gozzi arrived with King and came over to us with an umbrella. "This should not take too long, Signorina," he said, handing her the umbrella. "I would suggest you not come in. It can be . . ."

"No, no, that's fine. We'll wait here."

Seeing Rinaldi going inside, Gozzi gave her a nod and went after everybody else. King trooped along dutifully.

"What's the cutoff line for being a Signorina?" she asked, opening the umbrella and handing it to me. "If you're not married."

"I always figured around thirty-five. Or when your looks go to hell."

"Thank you very much."

"So be flattered. He's still calling you Signorina."

I had the umbrella, but she was leading—first around to the near side of the bunker, not quite as casually as she wanted to make it seem. "It's really a crypt, isn't it?"

"Yup. No windows to peek inside."

"Miss something for a change, Danny. It'll help me feel I have original ideas every so often."

We didn't say much more, instead trying to work up even a passing curiosity about the headstones spaced around the horseshoe gravel path separating the bunker from the rest of the plots. BELLINI, MOTTA, FAVRET, LATERZA, SONNINO, and LECCO had all passed away in the 1960s—that was one fact to be gleaned. Another was the name LECCO—Camilla Borgato's family name, according to Piero Milano. Was there any particular Milano didn't know about the extended Borgato clan? Yes, came the surprisingly swift answer: Whatever it was he hadn't told me yet. And there *was* something. At bottom, in fact, hadn't Piero Milano's encyclopedic, shouted tales been something like Alicia Silvestri's walls—all jumble meant to distract?

King finally appeared in the entrance of the bunker. He looked over at Winans, who had also had enough of the car and was now standing near his window and gave a small nod. "What does that mean?" Barbara asked, her anxiety back in full. "And why is he telling Winans before he tells me?"

Because Johnny Iler—hypochondriac English teacher and certainly not some CIA spook—had ceased being important.

| 30 |

THE RELIEF WAS like a sliver of air that didn't belong—a cold draft in the heat that didn't cool enough, a warm current not strong enough against the cold. Driving back to the hotel, the efforts by King and Winans to be tactful only made it worse. Whether they were telling Barbara they could only guess at the turmoil she had been through or were relaying Gozzi's assurances the body would be ready for shipment to New York within 24 hours, there was the hovering translation that their responsibilities were all but at an end and that the personal was no longer going to be able to hide behind the official. Barbara sat stonily in the back looking in dire need of more of the official. She didn't really say anything until after we had gotten out of the car and were walking into the hotel lobby. "I think we better call Alicia and tell her," she said. "I should be the one to call, don't you think?"

"I think so."

She got her key from the deskman, and I got my key and a big manila envelope. "A signorina left this for you," the clerk reported. "She said you were expecting it."

There was no return address on the envelope, but I knew what it was. I could picture Nino sitting outside in the car while Flavia entered the hotel and walked over to the desk with her glossies. In fact, I could picture Nino anywhere except out at the cemetery. Nino Borgato was

somebody who always made good on the promises he presumed others
would deliver on.

I didn't know where to start thinking about Barbara, so I chose the
path of least resistance—King's passing remark in the car that she could
be on her way back to New York "tomorrow—or the next day, if you
prefer" and her meek but noncommittal "yes." By supposing she would
go for the "or the next day, if you prefer," I didn't have to think we had
merely a few hours left together and could afford to catch up with my
wits alone for a while. And how about this for a novel idea: After all my
whining to Minton about how unfeasible it would be, why not file my
opening story?

"Of course," she said, as we waited for the elevator. "I didn't realize
how tired I was. I'll call Alicia and then get some sleep."

I called Cleary from my room. He sounded higher than his tea regimen would have accounted for and had a storm of questions. I answered
a couple in exchange for the address of the office where I could file. He
did some cackling over his foresight about the Borla body and promised
to call ahead to the office for me. I hung up before he started asking
about the still-missing Nullo Borgato.

The filing office was behind the Trevi Fountain. The rain had stopped,
and the air was one with my dank meditations as I walked over to it. The
most obvious answer about the Borgato body, of course, was that it was
still on some hospital slab somewhere with Borla's name attached to it.
The second most plausible solution was that, with Borla's name on it, it
had been shipped off to a potter's field, not to be discovered again until
some developer came along to claim the land for more high-rises, bars,
and laundromats. Would Gozzi do anything to halt that lazy process?
I couldn't see it. Like King, he had felt satisfied with his good deed in
discovering Iler.

Which seemed to bring everything back to Nino. Even Gozzi would
have had to overcome his dread of tangling with the Dottoressa Gallo if
the Borgato family began pressuring him. But Nino hadn't exactly been
showing consistency on that score. Just what the hell was going through

the asshole's mind—aside from stringing along Flavia's singing ambitions? It was as if he had known Iler was going to turn up in his father's grave!

And then there was something else: If there was anything at all to my fantasies, if Piero Milano had been even minimally serious about the reasons Borgato had for dropping out of sight, it could not have been a one-man trick. Borgato would have needed some major connivance from someone at the hospital—somebody in a position to falsify not only casket nameplates, but medical charts and death certificates. And that was a toughie for my mental ramblings. Nullo Borgato sounded like a lot of things, but not like some member of the Odessa with a vast network to help him disappear. Nobody seemed to have *cared* about him that much.

| 31 |

THE FILING OFFICE was on the second floor of a palazzo belonging to the Italian news agency. It was a windowless, oblong affair with two trestle tables and four computers. A 40ish woman with ginger bangs looked up from her keyboard as I walked in. "You're Cleary's friend? I'm Madigan. You can use that one over there. Just make sure you write down your billing number in the log before you leave."

The billing charges reminded me of Annie's call. So what had been so important she had needed to contact Minton, but then hadn't bothered to call me at the hotel?

"Make a note of that, too," Madigan sang as I punched out my home number. "You don't account for it, one of us is going to get stuck for it."

Maybe she just shouldn't have sounded so chirpily distrustful as I was calling to talk about whether my cracked brown loafers should be boxed or thrown out. But Madigan suddenly felt like the answer to some healthy rancor. "What's your first name?"

"Vicki. Why?"

"And I bet you use both names when you're signing off on a credit card charge, right? You're not some mythical 'Madigan,' you're Vickie or Victoria Madigan. You don't break the clerk's balls."

"I don't understand."

But Annie did, I thought, as her tentative voice came on the line. Annie knew not to look for some neutral observation in my most obscure remarks when I was trying to be offensive. The offense was all. If nothing else, our marriage had been good for that.

The news was more urgent than a how-are-you: Joe McAteer had been dropped by a stroke while sweeping his kitchen floor. He was paralyzed down his left side but was otherwise hanging on. Annie had been at the hospital for most of the last 24 hours, and I had caught her only because she had dropped home for a shower and change of clothes. "They say his chances are fifty-fifty. His heart and lungs seem okay, but there's been a lot of damage. They won't even know how much until he's well enough for a more thorough examination."

What were the next words? I wanted to lean over Madigan's shoulder and borrow some of the ones she was typing. "Want me to come back?"

She took as long to say no as I had to ask the question; and it wasn't even a clean no, at that. "There's nothing you can do except sit around here, and you have your job. How long you think it'll be?"

I had Barbara's schedule, of course—36 hours or so. And then there was Minton's timetable—two or three days max. And not to forget Nullo Borgato's—forever or until I found out what had happened to him, whichever came first. Only my own schedule seemed to have been misplaced. "A couple of days. But if you need me back tomorrow, I could probably get a flight out."

She had heard enough reluctance to confirm her suspicion. "That would be crazy," she sighed. "It could go on like this for weeks, the doctors said. Just do me a favor and call tomorrow? I have the number of the desk on the floor where he . . . "

And like that, we were sliding safely down into practicalities, into numbers, into times. It seemed too easy even to me. "You can't sit there by yourself all day, Annie."

"That's what you do, Danny. Unless you have a better plan." There it was again—the *plan*. "Connie's ringing the bell. She's driving me back to the hospital. Call me tomorrow."

She didn't wait to hear another ambiguous answer, just hung up. Madigan was waiting for me, now showing nothing of the telephone sentry. "Bad news?"

"My father-in-law had a stroke."

"I'm sorry."

"Thanks."

She still didn't turn away; she wasn't exactly looking at me, but she seemed to need me standing in front of her to locate something at the edge of her thoughts. "Don't you think there's a kind of divine hint in it when people start dying but don't actually die right away?"

"Excuse me?"

"A divine hint, yes," she said, nodding to the completion of her thought. "Like we still have time to make up with the person dying, work out some idiot misunderstanding we've had. Otherwise, why didn't the person just die? I think Jesus lets people die in stages as a way of giving those around him a second chance."

I didn't laugh; a muscle and a tendon or two thought about it, but I didn't really want to. What I mainly wanted to do looking into Vicki Madigan's zealous glint was to stop thinking about death, stop knowing people associated with it, and stop conceding it even existed. The McAteers, the Ilers, the Borgatos, the Borlas—get away from all of them. *That*, I thought, was my plan.

| 32 |

BUT YOU CAN'T do that very easily. First, there are all your physical surroundings—broken chairs, ancient computers, inkless pens—that drag
you right back into all that Ecclesiastes talk about there being a season
for everything and guess which one this is? Then there are your gathered
facts about wrong bodies being shipped across the Atlantic, other wrong
bodies substituting for the originally wrong ones, and right bodies showing up in wrong graves. At best, the payoff is a largely complimentary
call from your editor but with a glancing shot that "your last two graphs
are a little dead." In short, for all your born-again intentions, you end up
even *writing* death.

"We a little sensitive tonight?" Minton asked.

"Maybe."

"Too bad. Sensitive we leave to the Letters to the Editor. Never mind
those graphs, I'll do them myself."

"Thanks, Ed."

"We're not spooling, are we?"

It had been another lecture topic at The Ink, that much I remembered; the rest, nothing.

"Spooling, like human beings do," he prompted. "You follow out
this line wherever it leads you because you're going to get smarter and
smarter going where it goes."

The bastard had been eavesdropping again. "Sounds like kind of a natural thing to do."

"And it is," he said far too amiably. "For human beings. But you're not over there as a human being, you're over there as one of my reporters. And we frown on spooling, Danny. It's far too timeless. Every deadline we nail down things, seal them shut, cut the fucking spool. You want to start paying it out again the next day, go right ahead. But only up to the next deadline. Am I getting across? Good. I expect a follow-up same time tomorrow. Now go get some sleep."

I did what I was told. Only when I was climbing into bed did I focus again on the whimsies of the moment, opening the envelope Flavia had left for me. Her full name was Flavia Bersenetti (recommendation: change it simply to Flavia), she had made a record of something called "*Siamo Insieme*" that was awaiting release (recommendation: change it to sold more than 100,000 copies), and she had been a semi-finalist at the cut for the most recent San Remo Festival (recommendation: change it to finished fifth, just out of the money). She was 24 (good), liked Madonna (recommendation: Spears or Aguilera), and preferred to sing about love rather than social issues (recommendation: except when she preferred to sing about social issues instead of love). There were five color shots. Three of them showed her on the same tiny bandstand with two guitar players, looking like an Italian strung out Juliette Lewis. A fourth was a head shot with naughty eyes. The fifth showed her laughing with an elderly, plump blonde who was identified on the back as a popular Italian singer of the 1950s and 1960s; in the background was Nino Borgato, his eyebrows raised to the camera as though to underline that he alone had been responsible for bringing together the recording queens of yesterday and tomorrow. There were a couple of other people trying to get the cameraman's attention, as well, but I didn't think either of them was Nullo Borgato. I would need to do some more spooling to be positive one way or the other.

| 33 |

I HADN'T LOOKED closely enough at some of the people standing around the Borgato grave with Gozzi. Either one of the cops had hidden a camera inside a uniform button or there had been a photographer on the scene shooting the casket being raised. I found the results of his work below the fold of the front page of two Italian papers the next morning. Both accompanying stories were big on words like *scandalo* and *errore*.

I took the papers up to Barbara's room, where she was at work with the help of coffee and sweet buns. She didn't need reminders of the pilgrimage out to the cemetery, so she took one look at the papers, threw them on the bed, and returned to the table where she had been writing and eating. "Have a coffee."

"You look like you're in the middle."

"Jack Nicholson got further in *The Shining*. Wendy the Wren just won't fly. I think it's because she doesn't know if she really wants to fly."

"Maybe you're forcing it."

"I have a deadline," she said tartly.

Plot the ambivalences. She dropped her pen on the legal pad and gazed out the window, wanting to be away from Wendy the Wren. She waved her hand at the extra coffee cup, wanting me to be company. She put her foot back up on the other chair, not wanting me *that* close as company.

"Write your story?"

"Part of it. Minton wants more."

"Can I see a copy?"

"Sure. Want me to go downstairs and get it?"

Another imperious wave—this one at me or at whatever goblin had predicted I would have answered differently. The fact was the part I had sent Minton wasn't the problem. The next part, where Iler slipped into the background behind Borgato, that was the part the goblin had been right to warn her about. "Mind if I ask a question?" she asked the Villa Borghese treetops. "When did you lose interest in Johnny?"

Percussion time was rattling my cup on my saucer and imagining her using my skull as cymbals. And when all the clatter had stopped, I still had more than one silence staring out the window. I truly didn't know whether she was referring to Borgato or to herself as the competition.

"It was a story and a free trip to Rome, right?"

"The way it started."

"When did it become more than that?"

When frozen into cowardice, I could hear Minton coaching, go with the truth. "I'm still not sure it has."

She played it back for herself, neither moue nor sulk, just a neutral observer of the Villa Borghese greenery, then nodded. "Okay."

But of course, okay was the last thing it was. "Part one," I said, deciding to go after *both* of brother Johnny's rivals, "I've got local folklore with Nullo Borgato. He's Don Quixote who falls off his horse before he even sees a windmill. Does he sound heroic in some asinine way? Yeah, maybe he does. More fascinating than Johnny? Yeah, sorry, but he does. I've heard nothing about your brother that didn't add up to this manic depressive who assumed he was interesting because he was breathing. The only funny thing I've heard about him was what you told me about that 'I'm sick, I'm dying' ploy to pick up women. Or maybe you made that up because even you need something more where he's concerned, that's why you can even give a second thought to Heckle and Jeckle's bullshit about the Our Man in Rome." She looked back at me with an accusation, but then seemed to forget exactly what it was. "Borgato, on the other hand, he doesn't seem to have ever gotten anything straight, life *or* death, and I think that's an impressive achievement."

I couldn't tell which of her expectations I was upsetting—miserably there was no question, empathetically I could always hope, fatally bet on it. So I just kept going, fast afraid Minton's belief in truth should have been confined to worship services at The Ink. "Part two, you. Logistics don't matter, whatever Wendy the Wren wants to think. You live in New York, I live there. If we want to go on seeing one another when we get back, no problem. But we're not worried about logistics, it's plain old geography that's scaring us a little. Has everything that's happened between us been because we're over here in some artificial dimension? I don't think so, I don't want to think so, but how can I know as long as we're here? Would I have called you again after that first day in your apartment if the two of us had never come here? I think so, I would like to think so, but that's too easy to say. I'm so new to my separation I haven't even started bouncing before we get to rebounding. Who are you? You're a beautiful woman with a lot of elegance, a lot of anger, a lot of ambition, and a lot of timidity, and I love making love with you. Skip the elegance and you should have discovered all those virtues in me, too. More than that I don't know what to say."

She did, and I didn't know whether it was the elegance, the anger, the ambition, or the timidity talking. She just reached over and pinched the sleeve of my shirt, not taking her eyes off her fingers, looking to see what the blue of the shirt told her about her unpolished nails.

"Alicia insists we have lunch with her," she finally said, her voice a whisper. "I know you don't want to. You've probably written everything about Johnny there is to write. But I'd appreciate it if you would come. Could you do that for me? Not for your story or for Johnny, but for me?"

It felt like the first thing I had done for her when I said yes.

| 34 |

MY FATHER HAD never been an especially funny man, but he had been addicted to one particular piece of slapstick. Whenever somebody referred to clearing one's head, he would screw up his face like an old Red Skelton nitwit, tilt his head to one side, and begin banging at his skull, gooning out: "Clear, clear, getting clear." Why that had struck him so funny I never figured out, but that was exactly what I felt like doing after leaving Barbara to a couple of hours of work before our lunch date. I didn't want to think as I started down the Spanish Steps, I wanted to tilt my head, stick out my tongue ga-ga-ga, and beat out all the worms inside, maybe watch them go crawling this way and that, causing a panic among the tourists catching the morning sun. Unfortunately, though, I got down the Steps without a single worm being set loose; worse, I realized when I saw the sign for the Via Babuino, another one had slipped into my ear. Six stores down the street, I found the name ALBERTO TORTOLA etched on the bottom of the glass entrance door.

Piero Milano had said gallery; what he had meant was high-ticket junk shop: all the pedestal tables, wardrobes, looking glasses, and vases I had last seen in one of Annie's "Masterpiece Theatre" shows. The silver that hadn't been gilded or burnished to a fault hadn't been polished for generations, making it look doubly authentic. One chalice near the door was big enough to have turned every priest who had ever used it into a drunk.

I assumed the balding, squat man sitting at a modern desk in the back was Tortola. He was writing in a ledger and was practiced enough in browsers to throw me only the vaguest of smiles. "I was told you had art. Paintings, sculptures?"

His smile bordered on a leer, but at least he was curious. "Who told you that?"

"Piero Milano. I think you know him through a mutual friend."

"Milano, Milano . . ."

"Elderly man. Wavy white hair. Friend of Nullo Borgato."

"*Ah, l'ufficio postale*! Yes, I remember!" He stood up to no more than 5'5" or 5'6" and came around the desk more recklessly than he should have with so many tables and shelves hemming him in; one of the newspapers with the Borgato grave picture on the front page was on the desk. "He was the one who told you I sold art?"

"Well, he said gallery, so I assumed . . ."

"We have a back room with some things, but it's decoration stuff. Make the room look better. I can't believe Milano told you to come here looking for art."

He laughed to give me another chance; I took it. "Actually, I was talking to him about Borgato. This story you've probably read about."

He managed to get everything from his shoulders to his knees into his sigh; only his expression remained skeptical. "These are the criminals we put in charge of things in this country! You're just relieved if it happens to somebody else, not you. You're an American, yes? You're interested in this teacher they found in poor Borgato's grave?"

"I'm trying to get some background on Borgato, too. Milano said you might be somebody to talk to."

He believed me and he didn't believe me, but it was enough for him to wave me into the visitor's chair squeezed up against the desk. "Why Milano says that I have no idea. But the little I know him; he seems to be somebody who likes hearing his own voice."

"But you did know Nullo Borgato."

"I don't usually go to the funerals of people I don't know. What do you want to know about him?"

"Well, I know he worked with you on a couple of things . . ."

"Milano told you that? Like I said, a man who likes to hear himself talk . . ."

"Not just him. Other people, too."

He supervised lacing his fat fingers together over his ledger; whatever he had been writing were words, not numbers. "I hope we're not talking about that *disgraziato* of a son," he said, pronouncing each word heavily. "But yes, in a business like this you depend on contacts. You hear so-and-so might be looking for this, so you ask people to find out more. Or they come to you and suggest buyers. I might have given Borgato a piece or two on consignment, yes."

"Did the sales work out?"

"Probably not, or I would remember. You can't be an optimist in this business. I always say expect little and you might be pleasantly surprised."

"So when a sale doesn't work out, the person who's taken the item on consignment gives it back to you."

"Of course. Otherwise, all these middlemen would end up with everything in here, and where would I be?"

We laughed at that together, and I felt more wonderfully sleazy than I would have felt in a hundred meetings with somebody like Charles King. Alberto Tortola not only didn't trust me (yippee!), he looked ready to unleash the dogs (yippee-ai-o!).

"So what does all this have to do with this American they found? Why should people in the United States be interested in Borgato? Hardly an exceptional man. The dreams and projects of a million others."

"But maybe a little less successful at them than you are?"

"This? I sell nothing for a week, then some Japanese tourist walks in and makes it unnecessary to sell anything for another week. It accounts for my time. I have no family to worry about. I don't have to count every euro. But time—that still demands attention."

As long as Minton wasn't around, I had no reason not to throw the dice. "My paper wants to know what happened to Borgato's body. I'll tell you the truth, I haven't been able to get a straight answer from anybody."

His mirth was convincing. "How can they tell you what they don't know? From what I read; the body could be in the Adriatic by now."

"That just doesn't seem like enough. If only for his family."

This time he didn't bother folding his fingers. "Whatever the son has told you, I would discount it," he said evenly. "There are several people I know who came close to giving the Borgato family two losses. Do you follow me, Signore?"

"Not really."

"This is what they call off the record?"

"If you'd like."

"I insist."

"Off the record, then."

He made sure the tables and closets were also agreed before coming back to me. "The first I heard about Nullo," he said more lowly, "it was a call from the son. Naturally, I was shocked. But then I was furious because this *drogato* says to me, 'I'm collecting money for a headstone for my father, but I can't afford it, so I'm asking all his friends to contribute a little to it.' Do you understand me? His father is still warm, but that's okay because he's found another way of financing his drugs! I know of at least three people he called with that approach, and he made a serious mistake because two of them are not people to be trifled with. Do you follow?"

I thought I did, though I wasn't sure he was one of the two people not to be trifled with.

"When I read this nonsense this morning, I had to laugh. Not only would there never have been a headstone, there would have been no body under it, anyway! It's the kind of absurdity . . ."

"Borgato would have appreciated?"

"That's right," he said, looking at me without edge for the first time. "Even to contemplate teaching the son of a bitch a lesson was a waste of time. Futility always takes the last card with the Borgatos!"

That thought had been more romantic when it was only mine. Hearing it from Tortola felt like a push back out to Fiumicino and New York.

"Sorry if I shock you," he said, not sounding at all sorry. "That kid insulted my intelligence. And I'll tell you whose fault that is—the father. Nullo was a sweet man, but he expected people to put up with him all the time, too. He'd have a buyer for this, a buyer for that—but never a sale! Like I say, I always expect the worst. But he had this sincerity that could get to you in a weak moment. What can I tell you? He wasn't much of a salesman getting rid of things, but he was very good at getting me to give them to him in the first place. I suppose we all have our weaknesses. Mine must be self-delusion and sincerity."

If the owner of a Fifth Avenue electronics store had looked at me with the same hypocritical resignation toward the world and all its mysterious contents, I might have said: *"Is that right? Yeah, it must be really hard on you having all these suckers get their CD players home, realize half the parts are missing, then come charging back in here demanding a refund."* But Tortola didn't run a Fifth Avenue electronics store; he was another few feet in my spooling to Nullo Borgato. So, instead, I nodded sympathetically that he could recognize so much human frailty. It was a miracle I had enough brains left to ask him how much Borgato had stuck him for.

"In what way?" he asked, giving himself a second to think.

"Well, the things he took on consignment, you must have had some general idea what they might have been sold for."

Up went the short arms. "Such questions! What difference does that make now? And what does that have to do with finding out where this missing body is? You ask questions like the Finance Police."

I decided on one more nifty lie before leaving. "I'm just curious because he seems to have died owing so many people money."

"Oh? Who else?"

"People who also asked me to keep their remarks off the record. And I will. It's just that he seems almost lucky to have died when he did."

I would have expected anything but what he did: blessed himself like the most superstitious of villagers hearing about a vampire on the loose. "Madonna, don't say such a thing! Death is many things. But luck? I don't think so."

And that was where it should have ended—with me having to admit that, instead of some cut-throat Peter Lorre, Tortola was, at most, a penny-ante smuggler who sometimes succeeded and sometimes didn't succeed in raking a few dollars off merchandise that had fallen off a truck in the Alps. Except that, as soon as I thanked him and stood up, he decided to force me to play out my lame opening gambit. "Who knows?" he laughed, waddling his way through his lamps to a back room. "You might find something perfect for your living room in New York. I have landscapes, fruit in bowls, peasants looking crushed and exploited in front of their huts. And angels—lots of angels."

The back room was more like a furnished cellar bin. The still lifes not stacked five- and six-deep on the floor had been hung helter-skelter on glaring red wallpaper that looked like it had come from a bordello.

"Decoration, not art. Art you don't want to see over your couch every day. It can disturb you. This stuff you stop noticing after a while. It just covers up the blank spaces. Tell Milano that when you see him. Tell him I don't have his airs about what I have in here."

I started to object he was making too much of my misinterpretation of the word gallery. But the three pictures framed over one another in the far corner of the room shut me up. I couldn't imagine Alicia Silvestri ever being happy about having her woodland gnomes described as mere decoration.

| 35 |

CONNECTING BORGATO AND Iler even vaguely was my first scoop
and impressed nobody. When I told Barbara about it on the way to Alicia's, her tight nod said she had heard everything about Nullo Borgato she
wanted to hear. I took that to mean she would also prefer being out of
earshot when I brought up the subject with Alicia. That moment came
when she left us in the kitchen while she fixed the table for lunch out on
the balcony.

Alicia acted fascinated mainly for my sake. "What a terrible coincidence! I must have even known this Borgato! Probably at Tortola's. He's
always having these little parties for this and that. He buys a mirror from
some estate, and that's all the excuse he needs to open champagne for 50
people. You wouldn't know it to look at him, but Alberto's a very sociable
person. I'm sure I must have met Borgato at one of those things."

I had absolutely no clue about where the dissembling stopped and
the dithering started, or whether there was even a difference between the
two. "What about Johnny? He ever go to Tortola's with you?"

"A couple of times. I think we should throw in more pasta. Better
to make too much than not enough. Johnny really didn't like Alberto.
Called him a . . . geaser?"

"Greaser."

"Like a scum?"

"Close enough."

She scrunched her eyes up against the steam rising from the pasta pot. "I think he was wrong. Johnny was too quick with first impressions. Alberto even took the paintings you saw because Johnny was grumbling about the things he was selling. So Alberto challenged him, asked him what things he should be selling instead. And without hesitation, Johnny said . . ."

She gave me a full display of her beefy back for a moment, and I thought what she wanted me to think: Boiling water can make the eyes tear.

"I really didn't want to give him anything," she finally said with a sniffle, "but how could I say no after Alberto agreed? Johnny would have looked foolish. So I picked three pieces I didn't like. He hasn't sold them? Well, he promised to take them, not sell them. I'll see if I can remember this Borgato better for you."

We left it at that until halfway through lunch on the balcony. It was an awkward table: the food, the weather, the conversation—they weren't off exactly, but they all seemed to need one more push to be enjoyable and, even with the help of wine, were clearly not going to get it. When Barbara said yes, she wouldn't have minded her sweater against the nagging coolness, Alicia pretended not to mind the veiled criticism of her decision to eat outdoors and I didn't mind getting up from the table to go into the living room for the sweater. What else I didn't mind was the opportunity to take another look at the trolls covering the walls.

Two things I hadn't noticed before: all the tiny creatures were men and practically every one of them was in some stage of a smile. Blankness was as foul as the expressions got, even on a couple who appeared to be tumbling off a log into a mud puddle. Alicia Silvestri's imagination was a placid little world; not even a hint of darkness unless you wanted to indict the paintings as a whole as some magnificent evasiveness. So what were those stories she wanted to keep so private? The only one that occurred to me right away was that bland Johnny Iler had been the perfect mate for her because he had never threatened her tranquility. Even with his death, all the essentials of her life remained intact.

I was already turning to go back outside when the second story occurred to me. Iler and Alicia hadn't had a one-way relationship, it hadn't been just to *her* benefit. And suddenly I felt I was in the company of Johnny Iler—scores of Johnny Ilers, some of them with red hats and some with green hats and some with brown clogs and some with black boots. Johnny Iler was prancing through the woods and picking cherries. Johnny Iler was fording a stream and reeling in a trout. Johnny Iler was pushing a rock into the entrance of a cave and tumbling down a hillside worried only about keeping the cap on his head. Johnny Iler, colossal wet blanket, without secret projects and without serious curiosity about those who had them, hadn't found his retreat in Rome or Italy or Europe, he had found it in all the demarcated panels of Alicia Silvestri's walls. The story I was looking at was *their* story: Johnny Iler finding his freedom through Alicia Silvestri's oils!

When I took Barbara's sweater back out to the balcony, Alicia was waiting with a melodramatic snap of her fingers and an amazed look of discovery. "He was a bald man! A very wide face! And he had a gold filling right here!" I hesitated behind Barbara to drape the sweater carefully over her shoulders, and not to see the annoyance I was sure was going to be there with another reference to Nullo Borgato. "Of course! From one of Alberto's parties, absolutely. Isn't it strange how you forget things until somebody keeps nudging you to remember them? Yes. He was a man without mirrors."

Even Barbara was teased. "Without mirrors?"

"Whatever you call it," she said dismissively, going back to her plate. "Not one of those men who talks to you like he's always peeking at some mirror to see what he looks like talking to you. This Borgato, he was beyond that. Like it was too late for him to impress himself, so he might as well just plunge forward, talk, talk, talk, and who cared who took him seriously? He was refreshing in his poor way. I mean, he was so . . . false. But in a genuine way, if you understand me."

Barbara didn't. "Sounds like it should be one or the other."

Alicia laughed. "That's what Johnny would have said. Black or white. Night or day. He thought it was a virtue to keep his mind closed."

Kaboom, but not the right moment for it, so I got back into my seat between them as fast as I could. "I've never associated teaching with a closed mind," Barbara managed, syllable by syllable.

"Oh, you don't really call that teaching," Alicia scolded lightly. "'Where is the bathroom?' 'How much is this Coca-Cola?' It was just another way for Johnny to rest his brain for whatever the next life might need it for. I'm thinking of Borgato. The man was a fraud without frills. Not because he wanted to cheat you, but because he'd gotten used to cheating himself. Like I said, he had no mirrors."

She went back to her wine as though she had said her last word on the subject. I kept my eye on Barbara's right hand, the one next to the carafe. But it didn't move. I thought of what Winans had said on the way to the nightclub about all the Ilers having the same passivity gene. He had been right: It *was* disconcerting she didn't go after Alicia's cruel summation of her brother. Whatever the dwarfs and their creator had had between them, no matter what feelings Alicia might have been keeping to herself about Iler, Barbara didn't know about them. All she knew was the crack about resting his brain for the next life. That should have been worth at least a shattered carafe of wine. But she did nothing but pick up her knife to cut her tough beefsteak into a smaller piece.

"By the way," Alicia said, "if there's anything of Johnny's you'd like to take with you, please say so. All I ask is you don't take your books back."

"He has my books?"

"Every one of them. All those funny animals and things. Some he even had to pay outrageous prices for at the English bookshop here. But he has a whole bookshelf full of them. I know! Let's make a trade! You leave your books and I'll give you a painting and anything of Johnny's you want."

"Why would you be interested in my books?"

"They were important to him," Alicia said, as though it should have been obvious," and I would like to keep something that was important to him. I really can't think of anything else."

| 36 |

I DIDN'T LET Barbara get out of the house without the promised painting. She had dismissed the offer the moment it had been made, but I
waited only until she announced it might be time to go to ask if there was
one piece on the wall that attracted her more than others. What I hadn't
expected was that Alicia would look equally put out by being reminded.
No one seemed to have meant anything.

Alicia's compromise was to choose something not from the living
room gallery but from the closet of her studio at the back of the apartment. Her reasoning was invulnerable: the three dwarfs watching a
fourth one belly flop into a waterfall was no more than 10"x12", making
it "easier to carry back to America." It would have been a more graceful
offering if she hadn't rolled up the canvas as though bestowing last year's
calendar and if Barbara hadn't accepted it as though assuring her hostess
it was no trouble at all dropping off some garbage downstairs on the way
out.

As for the offer of taking something of her brother's, Barbara settled
on a magnetic pocket chess set she had apparently given him years before.
"You seem to have gotten more out of her than I did," she said coolly in
the cab back to the hotel.

"Maybe you could've gotten more if you'd asked."

"That's not what I meant."

"It's what I mean."

"Don't tell me you can't figure it out. Johnny was a roomer there. Just sometimes he and the landlady did things together."

"Like screwing?"

"You don't have to be coarse."

"Actually, I think they had more than that. I think they had a living arrangement of convenience. I think they were both misanthropes joined together so as not to have to bother with third parties."

"The lady with the elves? A misanthrope?"

I didn't know why, but I wasn't surprised she didn't object primarily to having her brother described that way. "You don't have to hate people to hate them. You can also just keep them unreal, all the way down in the lowest recess of your soul. You can turn them into plastic sets of Smiley and Grinny and Happy Moe."

She blinked me back into focus the way she had that first day in her East Side apartment. Maybe it should have been comforting she knew exactly what I was talking about, but it wasn't. I really didn't want Walter Wiggly pondering whether I was going to turn out to be just one more enemy in a lifetime of them.

| 37 |

MARTIN ST. CYR was coming out of the hotel as we drove up. He had just left a note informing Barbara that Iler was owed money by his school and that the director counted on being able to hand it to her personally. Heckle delivered this news through an empty cigarette holder in his mouth and with the air of nudging her to join him in appreciating some drollery. I left her to decide about going with him and entered the hotel. The clerk didn't have any more pictures of Flavia for me, but he did have two messages—one from Cleary and one from Piero Milano. Both had obviously read the morning papers.

My first call was to Annie; not only wasn't she home, she had forgotten to turn on the answering machine. Since that seemed like an unprovable fulfillment of my promise to call, I went through Queens Information to the hospital, only to be stopped there by a night nurse who reported no sighting of "Miss McAteer." I left my name with the nurse wondering if New York State had passed a divorce law in the last 48 hours that was even speedier than the one in Nevada.

It was only afternoon, but again Cleary sounded like he had been lacing his tea. What he had apparently been doing before that had been looking at his options. "It's fair game now, right? Everybody's on this thing and I've had a few inquiries from some of my other employers."

"Tell me what you want and what you got, Fred. In any order."

He laughed; and tried to sound canny about it. "Well, I am assuming I'll see a check for services rendered. And I have nothing against staying with you."

"Minton knows everything. And anything else I'll put in writing."

"Good. I prefer dollars. Not that these euros aren't a lot more attractive than kroner and francs. . . ."

"Fred?"

"Right. Lamberto Borla has no immediate relatives. He used to be an actor. Did Shakespeare in South America regularly. Some said it was a front for darker dramas."

"I don't care about Lamberto Borla, Fred."

"That's what you said last time."

"I'm saying it again."

"Okay. The other two. I think I'm really on to something. But I'd prefer not talking about it on the phone."

Of course, he did, I thought: That would give him time to be garroted before I got over to see him. "Okay, we'll meet. I have to file again in about two hours. One question."

"What?"

It seemed like giving away my best card, but I didn't see much of a choice. "Whatever it is you have, is it going to contradict the possibility that Borgato's still alive?"

I can't say I hadn't known his answer would have excited me, but when he said, "On the contrary," I couldn't help punching the pillow in glee.

| 38 |

I WENT FOR Milano as soon as I hung up with Cleary. When you're on a winning streak, you don't want any games postponed—or even the time to worry about how they might be. Then Milano's instant anger made me rethink that philosophy. "You were playing me for the fool!"

"I knew nothing. I was just speculating, remember?"

"You knew Borgato wasn't in that grave!"

We went around that bush a couple of more times. Finally, about a second before I lost my patience at having to defend myself, he started losing some air in his balloon. He was still aggrieved, but also trying to sound conciliatory in saying: "So what you need now is my wise counsel."

"I do?"

"It's very simple. If the man did go through this charade you say he did, he wants to be left alone. Do you want to take that away just to write another newspaper story?"

"You're assuming a lot more than I am, Piero."

"And you're not answering my question. Is another newspaper story, one for thousands of Americans who don't care one way or the other about any of this, is that worth sabotaging what the man might have done?"

Sabotaging? Maybe it had a lighter meaning in Italian than in English? I didn't think so. Milano's strenuousness didn't admit many light considerations. I might have almost thought he was protecting not just some elaborate disappearance worked out by Nullo Borgato, but a very real Nullo Borgato sitting somewhere near his telephone.

"You're the one who sent me to Tortola and gave me those other names, Piero."

"You went to see Tortola?"

The question hung like dogshit on my shoe: Whichever way I moved was only going to make matters worse. "He didn't act all that put out. Made it sound like Borgato only cost him pennies."

There was a grunt and nothing else. I still wasn't ready to accept every sign and fantasy in front of me, though, so I gave him another chance to head off Cleary, to drive them all away. "What do *you* think, Piero?"

"I think you're right," he said, sounding incredibly sad as he hung up.

| 39 |

WHAT DID I owe Nullo Borgato? He had headaches with his son, debts with Tortola and others, maybe a thousand other unresolved commitments? Excuse me, but none of that was exactly like having buttonmen on his trail. On the other hand, if he really was still alive, he had been responsible for putting Barbara through all her anxieties about Iler. I knew Barbara, didn't know good old Nullo. Who had a stronger claim on my sympathy?

Weighed down by these profound questions and by Alicia's wine, I nodded off on the covers for a half-hour. When I woke up, I had another mouthful of reasons for not feeling energetic about anything. Feeling more conscientious than conscious, I scribbled out a few lines on my notepad for Cleary to present to Minton as a voucher for services rendered, brushed my teeth, and headed for the Foreign Press Club. The late afternoon chill felt like something Alicia had sent after me from her balcony.

Cleary was sitting at the Foreign Press Club bar with a heavyset, raven-haired woman. She was listening to him more intently than I had ever had the feeling of doing. Was that why his scoop on Lamberto Borla was still the only one on the scoreboard? He introduced me to the woman, Felicia Canton, with enough exuberant swings of his arm to sound like he was ordering a round for everybody. In fact, he was, and I was paying. "Set up enough appointments here, Fred, and you can drink free all night."

Cleary gave me a cackle of a laugh. All he needed was a dirty white linen suit and straw hat. With all the drinking he had evidently been doing lately, he was not only shaking bone, but smelly shaking bone. "Know the tactic, do you? Oh, yes, that place downstairs from your paper."

"The Ink. You were pretty good at it one night."

"You have to make allowance for European salaries, Danny. Just like I make them for troops parachuted into my territory."

Felicia Canton shouldered her way between our stools with a stare she might have learned from "The Sopranos." She had things to ask and wasn't going to wait another second to do it. All the questions were related to the Spanish paper she worked for and to the career of Lamberto Borla. Borla, it seemed, had been part of a Shakespearian acting troupe that, by coincidence or not, had always left some South American backwater days before the local guerrillas found themselves with more guns, cash, or both. What could I tell her beyond that?

There were probably a hundred ways of telling Felicia Canton I found her information fascinating. The 101st way was gaping at her big teeth with another Belated Awareness.

"You didn't know any of this?" she said, making it sound like a felony charge. "Fred said you knew everything about this story."

As compensation for her disillusionment, I thought she deserved to be cut in on at least part of the Belated Awareness. "If you wanted to persuade somebody you knew a second somebody and you started describing this second somebody . . . Bear with me a second. When you got to his teeth, what would you say? To prove you actually knew this second somebody?"

She shrugged like a good but impatient sport. "He had none?"

"Okay. But next to that?"

She consulted with Cleary's puzzlement a moment, then brightened. "Gold! A gold tooth!"

"Drink up. You've just earned another one."

"You don't believe people can have gold teeth?"

The question was, had Alicia Silvestri also made up the details about Borgato being bald and having a big face? "What I believe is that some people are so opposed to dealing with conflict they can't even stand it in somebody else's mind. I believe they'll say anything at all to make the conflict disappear because that way it will also disappear from their lives."

"Isn't that called lying?"

That one I didn't know. After all, if Alicia had been lying, it had been for me, to make me feel closer to my elusive object. How could such kindness be written off harshly as mere lying? All she had been telling me, at bottom, was that her stories and my story were the same bullshit, so why not dump another leprechaun off the log?

It took Felicia another sip of her Manhattan before she accepted, I couldn't help her with Lamberto Borla and two more after that to excuse herself for the ladies' room. Cleary watched her swing her big bottom on clicking heels all the way across the bar to the bathroom door before turning his seediness back to me. "You're serious about putting into writing my contributions to this story?"

I showed him what I had scribbled in my hotel room. His face said he had lost a bet with his distrust of mankind; he was so impressed he just left the piece of paper on the bar between us. "Only I have this so far," he said, making sure the bartender was gabbing with somebody at the short arm. "Borgato had what they call a relationship with an opera singer named Vivian Gertz. They apparently had a lot of messy scenes. But the biggest scene, I'm told, was after he took up with a new lady. Know her name?"

I gave him his moment.

"Paola Restivo."

"Yeah? So?"

"Name means nothing to you?"

"Fred!"

"Suppose I said Paola Restivo was a doctor?"

"Suppose you did?"

He looked absolutely delighted as he checked the door to make sure Felicia wasn't on her way back. "Guess what hospital Paola Restivo works in, Danny. Come on, give us a good guess."

I pictured an old scoreboard operator in Wrigley Field getting his orders to pull in the big number 1 next to Cleary's name and replace it with an even more ostentatious number 2. If the world were a fair place, I thought, staring at the sheet of notebook paper on the bar between us, Cleary would have been passing that written testimonial to me instead of vice versa.

So thank Christ the world wasn't a fair place.

| 40 |

MINTON DEMONSTRATED AGAIN he could always be ornerier than the world. He wasn't knocked out by all the official Italian bafflement over the switching of bodies, and certainly wasn't about to endorse rumors, suspicions, or just plain feelings that Borgato was still alive somewhere. He *might have been* impressed if I had tied Paola Restivo to something, but I hadn't so he wasn't. As for Cleary, there was a chance of an italic credit if his information yielded anything, but then again there was a chance of no italic credit. Getting right down to it, in fact, why didn't I hold my fire until I could say something concrete about Doctor Restivo one way or the other? Or put it this way: Get some copy out of Doctor Restivo in 24 hours, file that, and then we'll see about going any further, or throw in the towel and come home. Ciao.

Since Minton's grouchiness couldn't possibly have been because of the brilliant job I had been doing, I decided on my way back to the hotel that one of the office's anti-smoking Nazis had caught him in the act.

For following St. Cyr over to her brother's school, Barbara had been presented with a scroll saluting JOHN F. ILER for "fulfilling the highest mission of the Warner Institute—extending the communication skills of the modern citizen." The paper had been conferred on her personally by the school director, one Carl Warner.

"He was a cartoon! Somebody from a Marx Brothers movie!"

"German accent?"

"But from Luxembourg. He mentioned that about twenty times."

I stared at the scroll more than its cheap printing deserved because I didn't know what to make of her mood. I had knocked on her door just as she was about to get into the shower, and she was padding around the room clutching her bath towel to her chest in a dither about the scroll, her meeting with Warner, and some piece of paper where she had written down the name of a restaurant recommended by St. Cyr. With all the scuttling, though, went an effort not to look me in the eye and an exasperation that seemed to have to do with more than a Groucho Marx foil.

"About $330," she said, ransacking her bag for a check that finally floated out. "This is what the pompous ass was holding back on paying."

"If you believe Heckle."

"Why shouldn't I? Warner was just afraid all this attention would show him up as a cheat."

I recognized the coals in her eyes, the snap in her voice, and the silence that dared me to dowse them. Once upon a time, when we had still cared, Annie and I hadn't needed much more to get into it for the whole night. "Cash the check as soon as you can. Make it money, any money, not specifically something to do with Johnny."

"What'd you think—I was going to put it on my wall?"

"Maybe just keep it in your bag awhile so it could gnaw at you every time you looked at it."

"Go to hell."

I went to the bathroom instead. When I came out again, she was sitting with her head on the backboard of the bed, still holding the towel against herself with one hand and staring blankly at the check in the other. From the bathroom door I could also see Alicia's painting—sticking out of the trash can under the night table.

"You found out more about Borgato?" she asked.

"Less. I think Alicia was making up a few details."

"That gold filling business? Heavy-handed of her, wasn't it? My six-year-old readers wouldn't have believed it."

Before I could worry about being accused of being a five-year-old, I saw the wet beads in her eyes; they looked even more solid in the reflection from the bureau lamp. "You know who she was describing, don't you? Johnny had every tooth in his head. And the baldness! He'd lose a single hair and he'd be in crisis! He was also as thin as I am."

"What're you saying, Barbara?"

"She was describing her *anti-Johnny*!"

"That's nuts."

"I can't believe you finally missed something. That stuff about not acting like a man looking at himself in the mirror? That's all Johnny ever did! There could be just the two of us talking, but he'd always be darting looks around him, like he was modeling for some invisible cameraman. What Alicia was telling you, Danny, was that your friend Borgato, to her mind anyway, was the exact opposite of Johnny."

"For what?"

"Ask her. Maybe she felt sorry for you. Maybe she didn't like seeing you so unsure about everything. But Johnny certainly wasn't charming, wasn't funny, and certainly would never admit to being ridiculous, like this Borgato was supposed to. You want the truth, Danny? Johnny robbed you of everything but his own leaden presence. He was dying, don't forget. That was enough for him and should have been enough for you, too. You should have been satisfied comforting that, holding that. You should have wanted to help him through the night any way he wanted you to. Whatever proper morality said." One of the beads finally popped, right down her cheek. "Do you understand, Danny?"

For a second, made-for-TV movies was the extent of what I understood about anything. But not saying anything at all felt just as empty, seemed to add merely more shames to the silence. "Incest is what we call bugs," I remembered dumbo Charlie White telling our eighth-grade teacher Mr. Mathews, and Mr. Mathews had spent the rest of the period looking threateningly at me and Billy Buckley in the back for snickering too cannily.

"Alicia knows. I felt it as soon as she looked at me the first time we went there. And then all that crap about being a model on the beach. Like she'd always pictured my body in some way. I was appalled Johnny would confide in her. Then I thought it made perfect sense. She was safe.

She didn't count all that much to him. She was tucked away over here, and she didn't exactly let daily realities get her down. What was it she said about money that day . . . ?"

I sat gingerly on the edge of the bed; I didn't want to think about anything Alicia had said. For what? The more people had said to me, had even breathed to me, the more I had missed.

"We went to close down the house in Rockland County after my parents had moved to Florida. They left it up to us to do what we wanted with the place. We both wanted to sell it. Johnny was working at one of those dead-end jobs with a market research house, and I was trying to sell my first book. Both of us needed the money more than the house. We sold it to a fireman up there, and he gave us a few weeks to take out everything we wanted." She took a better look at the check. "This kind of money was a lot more important then. Do you think that's a sign of progress?"

There was no unawkward way to get across the bed to her, so I stayed put. I didn't need to think of her as a frail innocent to be horrified, but since I wasn't feeling horrified, it seemed easier to think of her as a frail innocent.

"He was coughing a lot. You or I would call it a cold, he called it dying. And the special occasion, of course. He couldn't let that go by without putting his morbid imprint on it. So much of our lives had been spent in that house. We couldn't pull a chair away from a wall without finding some indentation older than we were. I actually found a buffalo nickel under a rug. Naturally, that just got Johnny sneezing some more. The dust, the air, the rain, the wind, the snow—there wasn't a single thing since the first moment of Creation that wasn't in on the plot to kill him!"

"Why did you believe him?"

She nodded—too forcefully, shaking the other bead out of her eye. "Because it was dramatic. Because it explained why a genius like him couldn't find anything better to do than count up how many people drove Fords and how many Buicks. Okay, he was only 25, but you expect geniuses to show their stuff by then. Mozart and Liszt had their best years behind them by then, didn't they? He *had* to be dying. It was his only excuse."

I wanted to ask where or when the genius expectations had started, had their parents been some monstrous caricatures of stage mothers? But that would have made me sound like one of Ed Minton's minions, and I had stopped playing that role the moment I had stepped on the plane in New York. Besides, that wasn't what I wanted to know, anyway; what I really wanted to know was what would never be printed in an Ed Minton newspaper—how they had gotten around to fucking.

"We thought it would be fun to sleep in our old bedroom one last time. At least I did, for about a half-second. He warned me, Danny. He really did. The look he gave me when I suggested it, there was no way I could misinterpret it. I felt the heat right under my chin."

"Were you drinking?"

She smoothed the towel over her thigh, indifferent to the scroll she was crushing underneath it. "An attenuating circumstance? Thank you, but no. The only thing in the house was old vermouth, and I hate vermouth. Johnny drank some, but not much. I wanted to be taken, Danny. By sickness. By death. By thwarted genius."

"By Johnny."

"If you want to be technical."

"Because you had absolutely nothing else going for you?"

"Another dick?"

"If nothing else."

The glare came and went. "This wasn't about anything else."

"What about him? You didn't have this death aura. Where the hell was *he* coming from?"

I didn't know how mad I was until I heard the question bounce off the walls around the room. "I'm sorry I said anything," she said, looking down at her hands folded over her stomach.

"Where was he coming from, Barbara?"

Okay, she was beginning to regret having opened her mouth. But there was something else, too, in the insouciance she affected in puckering her lips and tilting her head at her hands: She had never felt it all that necessary to question what had driven Johnny that night. She was who she was, right? How could Iler *not* have wanted to screw her?

As infuriating as it was, it was the first time I had seen her confident about more than her ability to rattle the Charles Kings of the world. "Like you said today," she finally replied. "He didn't like people. Except for me, maybe."

On the way up to her room, I had stopped off at mine to get the copy of the story I had sent Minton. She had asked to see it; then had forgotten she had asked to see it. Feeling it in my jacket pocket was like feeling some old Kleenex that had gone through dry cleaning: I couldn't imagine how it had ever seemed useful.

"It was just that night," she said, back to daring me to look away from her. "Once because we both wanted it, the second time because we both knew we could never live in the same city again, let alone near each other, so there was nothing more to lose, was there? We never came right out and agreed not to see each other, it was just there. The next morning, it was like *everything* had been decided—what furniture we wanted, what we were going to sell, what we'd leave for the fireman, the Christmas cards and occasional notes we'd drop one another. He'd even made the decision he'd be the one to leave New York."

"And you never saw him again?"

A traffic cop blew a whistle somewhere outside. "Once. On Second Avenue. He was with these two idiots. They were the first Heckle and Jeckle. One of them insisted we get a drink. There was really no way out of it. So we go into this pub and these two start talking about these shirts they've just seen in a window. How the stripes shouldn't cost more than the solids, especially if they didn't have collar buttons. I swear to God, that's all they talked about. And Johnny, he was listening to them like they were debating the meaning of life! He even had opinions, Danny—opinions about whether window designers should lay out a single shirt or lay a few over one another to attract passersby!"

"Easier than talking to you."

"Of course. And being me, I let him get away with it until they all said goodbye and went walking down Second Avenue. I watched to see if he'd turn around, but he didn't. I guess he was too intent talking about what he'd seen in Florsheim's window."

"And that was it until all this business?"

She nodded her chin into her chest. "You can accuse me of being lazy in a lot of ways, right?"

"What haven't you accused yourself of since then?"

She knew the answer; unflinchingly. "Going to bed with somebody who counted so little even his lover thought of human things when she wanted to invent his exact opposite. Going to bed with somebody because she's as unreal as her little creatures. Will that do it for you?"

I thought it would.

| 41 |

SHE NEVER FOUND the scrap of paper with St. Cyr's restaurant tip, and neither of us missed it. We ended up in a *birreria*—blond hardwood booths, dark beer, black bread, goulash. If we didn't listen to the customers in the booths around us, we wouldn't have been in Rome. If we didn't listen to the thoughts behind every reference to "next week" or "after the burial service," we wouldn't have both lived in New York. Thanks to the goulash, we weren't even in the Germany of the beer garden's decor, but at some nonexistent crossroads between Germany and Hungary where it was up to us to make up the genuine.

We went back to my bed. She hadn't confessed to anything there. Canvasses, scrolls, and checks weren't littering the place. We were closer to the traffic, and it either had to sweep us along with it or have no impact on us whatsoever. She had never felt longer or thinner, never looked whiter, never smelled talc sweatier. There was a goal of going all night until she had to get ready for her flight, and then there was no more goal except not to be uselessly anxious. By two o'clock she was asleep next to me, needing more than my hand and the sheet against the night chill but refusing to move her arm so I could get to the blanket jammed into the footboard. I nodded off thinking about all the tourists who would be taking the plane with her in the morning, how they were probably right then resisting sleep in hotels across the city so they wouldn't have to regret having wasted their final moments in Rome. I felt happy she hadn't seen any need to resist.

| 42 |

CHET WINANS CALLED from the lobby a half-hour earlier than he had promised; he had had second thoughts about the traffic out to the airport. Already packed for an hour, Barbara was as grateful as I was. When we went downstairs with her bags, I found not only Winans signing something for the desk clerk, but Piero Milano sitting on a divan. I hadn't planned on going out to the airport for any lingering goodbyes anyway, but Milano's presence seemed to fill in a gap before one was created.

First, though, there were the gifts. Winans was toting an elaborately wrapped box for Barbara from the Kings that looked like Perugina chocolates. Then Chet handed her a memo pad in a leather casing embossed with the embassy seal—"so you can have good thoughts about us once in a while." It was the first time I could see Winans eventually rising through the ranks higher than King.

And then Barbara was handing me something. "How you've managed to know me this long and not start memorizing my works, I don't know. But maybe you can start with this."

The green-and-white cover said HENRIETTA THE HEN LOOKS FOR A NEW HOUSE and showed a hen leaving tracks behind her as she advanced on the entrance of a colonial mansion. The discoloring of the letters and black specks on the cover told me the book had come from Alicia Silvestri's during some ostensible trip to the bathroom.

"You will read it?" she asked, looking proud of her theft.

"Of course."

"Good. Thanks for everything. Bye."

It was only after she had kissed me on the cheek and was following Winans out the door that I registered her black dress. Clearly, she was going to be ready for any photographers at Fiumicino or Kennedy.

"Beautiful woman," Milano said. "She writes about *galline*?"

"For children."

"And who do you write for, *americano*?"

Back to reality. "What do you want, Piero?"

He made an attempt to shuffle uncertainly, but it was beyond him. Milano was one of those older men who seemed to radiate energy first thing in the morning—always walking a little too fast, talking a little too loud, and assuming everyone wanted to be in step with him. His peculiarity was a talent for keeping up the shouting part long after his other stamina had deserted him. "I thought you would like to talk to Paola Restivo," he said, looking like he too had ripped off a book from Alicia Silvestri. "So I called her and arranged for us to have a coffee together."

"How do you know her?"

"She happens to be a cousin of mine . . . No, I didn't introduce her to Borgato. I didn't even know they were acquainted until I visited him in the hospital."

That was all he volunteered until we were out of the hotel and climbing into a blue Fiat he had parked on the sidewalk two doors down. "I'm in the vanguard of giving sidewalks back to cars," he chirped. "Too much time spent on the priorities of the human race, don't you think?"

I didn't know what layer of the onion I had landed in. His self-assurance was all smarting—one that had probably started as soon as he had slammed the receiver down on our conversation the day before. "I'm going to say it again, Piero—I'm just guessing."

"So you're guessing," he said, dropping us into the street from the sidewalk with a bang that rattled through my stomach. "You're allowed."

He began humming as he maneuvered down the winding street. Had it been only a week since Joe McAteer had also dropped me down from a sidewalk in a car? It seemed like an insight into how elderly people measured years—so close and yet so far away.

| 43 |

WE WENT TO the same cafe behind the hospital where I had grabbed a sandwich after seeing the Dottoressa Gallo. The telephone directory I hadn't dared use to look up the Borgato family still hung off its wall chain; it seemed to have developed a mocking attitude toward me in a few days.

Paola Restivo was a tall, spindly woman about 50 with a bun at the back of her black hair, big eyes, and swept back cheekbones. She also had a rasp for a throat that sounded like too many years with Cleary's self-immolating cigarettes. She stood up immediately from her table to embrace Milano and shake my hand—not the anxious cordiality Alicia Silvestri had shown to me and Barbara the first time, but a spontaneous friendliness that didn't need Nullo Borgato or any other excuse for having a coffee with somebody she truly wanted to see. That the somebody was clearly Milano didn't matter; it seemed enough that the hospital across the street had more going for it than the Dottoressa Gallo.

"What do you expect?" she laughed after I had explained my face. "Gallo works with the dead all day. That leads to many one-way conversations, no?"

"Now that you mention it."

"I could never imagine such a profession. Now she is in shock because not only are her corpses talking back to her, but her superiors at the ministry want to know why she didn't listen to them!"

It was the first laugh I'd had at Gallo's expense that didn't feel alto-gether snotty. But Milano could have skipped it. "Our American friend has a crazy idea Nullo is still alive, Paola. What would you say to that?"

Her amusement before Milano's blurt wasn't practiced exactly, but she didn't feign any dismay, either. "I would feel put out," she said. "Nullo and I had been seeing each other. If he decided to live without telling me, that wouldn't say much about our relationship."

"As I told Piero, there are just . . ."

"He calls it a guess."

Now she thought Milano was the funny one. "And of course, that annoys you, cousin, because you can't imagine anyone keeping a scheme like that from you."

"He'd like to know if it's possible."

"This is a game we've been playing since childhood," she said back to me. "Which of us can discover the best secret about the other. My par-ents, for example, were secret voters for the monarchists. I knew about it, but I was ashamed they could be so anachronistic. I even preferred my friends to think they were Christian Democrats. But then Piero discov-ered the truth and lorded it over me."

Milano pushed a little more. "What he wants to know is if you're getting even with me by hiding Borgato somewhere."

She wouldn't let me look away. "My big discovery about Piero was his father. Piero was always shouting at him because he assumed the old man was deaf. Actually, his father had no organic damage at all, just a lot of wax in his ears. But he preferred to have Piero shout at him and think he was handicapped to going to a doctor and getting the wax removed."

"He was a proud man," Milano objected, apparently as much for himself as for his father. "But you're forgetting the question, Paola."

She hadn't been, of course. "Do you know what these guesses of yours amount to legally?" she finally asked. "For me?"

"Then they're wrong?"

In retrospect, I thought there should have been a neater line, a more dramatic bridge, leading up to that moment when she pressed her lips into the spume of her cappuccino, gained a bubbly mustache for a moment, then licked it away again. There had been my fantasy, there had been my suspicion—there just should have been something more official, more trumpeting, about the arrival of my certainty.

"Suppose I told you he was alive? You still haven't answered what Piero asked you on the phone last night."

Finally, half a point on the scoreboard. It hadn't been Borgato, it had been her, I had sensed hovering over Milano during our phone call. "It was a theoretical question when he asked it."

She relieved both of us by blinking. "I've been a doctor 24 years, Danny. Some patients I've had for almost 20 years. And sometimes it's like they are human graphs. They come to me with this or that problem, and I keep their line of success running across the top of the graph. But as the years go on, the line begins to sag here and there, and then at a certain point it may drop very close to the bottom. Even when I do something to get their line back up, we all know there will be another drop soon enough and I will probably be a little less successful the next time. It can be a very depressing way of viewing people. The only thing that keeps a good doctor going is the sheer number of graphs. Success with one, mild failure with another, total failure with a third. If you're fortunate, they all get a little mixed up in your mind, so it's not like your job is to chart lines from the top to the bottom. They call it mortality."

"Yes?"

I took her smile as congratulations for not collapsing in admiration before her vision of the Human Graph. "Mortality is inevitable," she tried again. "But that should really be the only thing that is. Why should we be miserable as we extend our line across the graph? Especially when there is not all that much wrong with us? Why be worn down to the bottom of the graph before our time by the greed and addictions of others? Why should we have to wake up every morning and have as our first thought, 'Oh. he's going to be calling me again today for this' or 'Oh, she's expecting me to meet her today at the lawyer's or the notary's or the police station?'"

"I thought that was part of the deal."

"Yes. But if there's an opportunity to get out of this deal?"

"To start a whole new series of bad thoughts in the morning?"

She liked that. "Of course. We're not talking about turning into angels or spirits here. We're just talking about easing some exhausting pressures that have gone on as a daily regimen far too long."

Minton, again: When flabbergasted, reach for the skeptical. "And Borgato's daily load, it was just so much more exhausting than everybody else's? If there was one person in the whole world who really needed to get away from bill collectors, it was Nullo Borgato?"

Both of them were disappointed in me. She consulted her cappuccino spoon, and he downed some prune-colored thing as though it were castor oil. "Even at the cost of jeopardizing you professionally and legally, Doctor?"

She didn't need my solidarity. "I undertake only what I believe I can succeed at. And it seemed worth the risk, yes."

"But it was *his* idea?"

They let that one pass: They seemed to have defined some hierarchy of admissions for themselves.

"He had to know the situation he was putting you in."

"Do I strike you as a child below the age of reason? Good. Then let's move on to what Piero asked you yesterday. Why does any of this interest you? You have your dead American back."

"The American was exchanged for this actor Borla, and that's where the mistake was," Milano seconded.

"Very nice, Piero. But there's still the Borgato tomb and missing body to explain."

"Not everything in life gets explained," he shrugged.

"Have you ever wanted to start over, Danny?" she pressed. "Really start over? It's a fantasy we all entertain now and then, yes? And the reason it remains a fantasy is because most of us have people, or maybe just routines, we are afraid to live without."

"And maybe we don't have the help to make it work."

"That too," she said, conceding little. "But imagine a case where none of those usual restraints are present. Somebody whose whole life has been an exasperation. People, including those in his own family, who at best have used their common blood to take, take, take, never give. Oh, you can delude yourself for a long time not even that matters, that underneath all the tiresome draining of your strength, there is that basic bond, that love which is just out of sight and that will be expressed . . . when? Tomorrow morning? Next year? You can go on waiting to reach that day for a very long time. You teach yourself to ignore all the continuing signs that maybe that tomorrow, that next year, will never be reached. Or maybe, you tell yourself, it will be reached on your deathbed, and *that* will make up for everything!"

"Okay, the whole world agrees Nino Borgato is a shit. But lay it all at his door? I don't think so."

"Of course not. And I'm sure by now you've had people tell you some of Nino's problems might have been averted if Nullo had been more of a father to him . . ."

Milano repositioned his legs with a grunt. "And Columbus would have discovered Japan if the winds had been different!"

"Please, Piero. And not just where Nino is concerned. If he'd been a better husband, maybe his wife wouldn't be living where she is. Has there been any relationship he didn't fail at? And the rest of it has been even more ridiculous! A man of poses. Of talking himself into jobs, situations, interests, even passions, for consuming his time!"

I didn't know what I was supposed to say before her sudden silence. The only thing that occurred to me as relevant was that she had been wrong about the relationship thing. Clarence Darrow couldn't have taken up Borgato's case so ardently. He certainly seemed to have impressed *her*.

"He's got more than that coming," she prodded.

"Because he didn't become a millionaire? Because people didn't take him seriously enough? Because maybe he wasn't even all that bright to start with? Look at it the other way, Doctor. He seems to have done an awful lot of things. Maybe he should have been grateful he got as far as he did with so little going for him!"

"You seem to know a lot about somebody you've never met."

I hardly disliked her; I even admired how she could disguise the mania of her self-assurance. And Milano, he was still the onion that got to me only when I let it. But they were also both beginning to rattle me with their smugness about doing only what any loyal apostle of the Chump Redeemer would have done. "Could we get back to the practical for a second, Doctor? You know, what everybody else is going to be doing while you're worried about me? Even if the cops are afraid of stepping on Gallo's toes, they're going to be forced into action. Some newspaper, magazine, or TV reporter is going to keep sniffing around. The story's just too good. You're not going to get away with it."

"This is your way of asking us to give you the story first?"

Scratch Milano's crassness, and I suppose it still was. "Tell me some reason *not* to write it, Piero. Screw my personal interest. I'm talking about it as something some plumber in Queens will get a kick out of before he turns to the sports page. Where else is my involvement here?"

He had no better idea than I did, and I was so satisfied with his look away that I didn't see her coming up on me from the other side. "Does what you know have to be what you write?" she asked.

Had I been asked that question since journalism school? For sure, when it had been asked in Ethics 101, it hadn't been for arriving at the answer she wanted to hear. "Meaning what?"

"Maybe if you understood everything . . ."

Milano clattered his chair back in protest; in a perverse way I agreed with him. "Understanding for the sake of understanding?"

"Is that so out of the realm of your profession?"

I knew what the Spooling theorist Ed Minton would have answered. For once, though, that didn't seem like enough of an answer.

| 44 |

MAYBE THE ODDEST part of our deal was that it didn't enthuse me more. For days, I had been running around treating Nullo Borgato as my personal Third Man, but once shown the entrance to the sewers behind the kiosk where Harry Lime had disappeared, I might have been trading off tidbits about some Brooklyn fire victim with the *Post* or Channel 11. And from any reasonable point of view, I did have something to celebrate. Not only had I nailed down the existence of a living Nullo Borgato ahead of every reporter between the North and South poles, but I hadn't had to undertake any commitments to go even further. Instead, though, the agreement felt a little like an admission I was wearing a watch and could check the time whenever I wanted.

Paola Restivo's offer was this: If I could hold off writing anything for another 24 hours, she would talk to Borgato about seeing me. If he couldn't make his own case for keeping things quiet, I would be free to write whatever I wanted. Milano listened to her proposal antsy about what two characters at the bar might have been overhearing. If the pair hadn't been there, he probably would have been paranoid about the *cornetti* sitting on the end of the bar. What remained of his calm departed altogether when I asked Paola how she had pulled off everything: He couldn't get up to the cashier fast enough to order another of his prune drinks.

"He really doesn't want me talking to you," she smiled.

"That's an understatement."

She lingered over Milano fondly for a moment. "The more practical the information I give you, the more incriminating it will be for me. That's what he's really worried about."

"He shouldn't be. If I write something, you'll end up having to go over it anyway. If I don't write anything, you're just telling me."

It was my own fault, but I could have done without her ready nod, as though she was already convinced, I wasn't going to write anything. I've always been better not making commitments when I was the only one not making them. I dared her to object to the pad I took out and stuck on the table. She didn't. If anything, she just found me more amusing.

Getting Borgato out of the hospital had been the easiest part. She had simply scheduled him for an X-ray, knowing he would be deposited in a corridor to wait his turn with several other patients. Then she had gone down the hall and, amid the self-preoccupations of the other patients about what their X-rays would reveal, escorted him off to a men's room around the corner where Milano had been waiting with a change of clothes. From there she had walked up to the mortuary, removed a certificate from a sheeted body on a gurney, and replaced it with her own.

"Borla?"

"There's the question," she said, shaking her head. "I would have thought so because Gallo has her little catalogue system up there. Bodies that are going to be claimed here to the left, those that aren't to the right. Reading about this actor, it should have been him. But what I didn't know about her system was that she reserved the same corner for bodies that weren't going to be claimed and those that would be shipped somewhere other than out the back door for a funeral. So I ended up putting my certificate on Iler's gurney. Or maybe Borla's. That part of the chaos happened without my help."

"But you took a certificate off the gurney . . ."

She shook her head and reached back for the bag she had twined around her chair. "I didn't look at it, just put it in my pocket and threw it away when I got outside. My guess is I put my certificate on Iler's body. Where the error on the nameplate occurred . . . You'll have to talk to Gallo's people about that."

"If I want to reconstruct any of this."

She pretended to be too busy leaving a tip to glance at the three or four words on my pad. "That's right. If."

There had been more than one misplaced body, and now there had been more than one bureaucratic foul-up. Walking back out into the sunlight with the Restivo-Milano family, I didn't have just one story, I had a whole series of them, not to write!

| 45 |

ON THE WAY back to the hotel, I bought as many Sunday papers as I could carry, figuring I would spend the afternoon assembling all the follow-up details Gozzi had leaked to the locals behind the backs of yours truly, Charles King, and the United States of America. I could have used another arm for the freight the desk clerk handed me. There had been calls from Annie, Cleary, and Alicia, and two from Nino. There was also a rolled-up painting of an elf jumping into a waterfall. "The maid found this in your friend's room," the clerk said, just this side of a smirk. "Perhaps it is something important she left behind and you could send her?"

Yes, perhaps I could, I thought, getting into the elevator; certainly, I wasn't going to dump it in *my* trash can and have the maid chase me out to the airport with it.

I tried Annie first, and again had to settle for the machine. I then called Minton, rehearsing several fragments of excuses about why he was going to have to stretch his budget for another day and even then, without any guarantee of receiving a piece. But sometimes the gods give you a bye. Only when Leo Rodriguez answered did I remember it was Sunday and that Minton was probably camped down in White Plains in front of his TV set. Normally, I didn't like Rodriguez (he was Frolich's pet), but I was ready to overlook that for not having to produce more stalling alibis.

"Yeah, he said there was an outside chance of something today, but Monday was more likely."

"I just wanted to be sure you knew that, Leo."

"Hey, if you've got something . . ."

"No, no. Monday's better."

"When you coming back?"

Whoops. "Miss me that much? Or is it Frolich?"

"Goodbye, Danny."

Goodbye, Leo Rodriguez. Hello, Ed Minton, and thanks. I thought about how the first time I had seen Minton out from behind his desk had been my third week on the job—at my father's wake. Before then, we had exchanged no more than a dozen words about anything but assignments, but he had walked into Sardi's Funeral Parlor the second night, come up to me and my Aunt Allie and shook our hands as though he too had lost at least a fragment of something. And then, even as I had been identifying him with title and everything else for Allie, he had fixed me with his watery eyes and said: "Your father would still be gone if I'd come here because you were on the staff 20 years. Keep gestures in perspective."

Who better to call with that thought in mind than the bad boy who hadn't lost his father as completely as he thought? For once, his coffee house sounded like it was hopping, and he sounded short of breath from actually serving tables. "My mother would like to see you," he said.

"Sorry. I don't have time for any trips . . ."

"She's in Rome. She read all that stuff and came down this morning."

"You haven't been making more promises in my name, I hope."

"No, no. She just . . . Well, come by tonight. She'll be here about seven. You can do that for a few minutes, can't you?"

Give Nino this: He was versatile enough so that even when you knew you were about to step into one of his cow patties, you were still curious to find out what breed of cow he had gotten to do his dirty work. And that didn't seem so far removed from what Tortola had said about his father.

I put aside the messages from Cleary and Alicia. I knew what he wanted and didn't have the foggiest idea about what she did, and that somehow made them equal for being put off. My sifting of the Italian papers produced little but rhetorical commentary, much of it of the sardonic persuasion. The ones that had gotten as far as the Dottoressa Gallo had come away only with ritual expressions of regret and pledges of in-house investigations. I would have liked to believe the coast was clear for meeting with Borgato, but it nagged me that Saturday night deadlines were probably the same the world over and that dailies saved their best weekend stuff for Monday. One paper also bothered me with a reference to "indications from ministry sources that the confusion around the corpse of the hapless teacher from America was merely the tip of the iceberg and that further inquiries would reveal deeper cases of incompetence, if not criminality." Was it a good or bad sign that only one paper carried that warning? I had no idea.

Neither did Henrietta. She was too busy looking for a new house before she was kicked out of her coop and didn't want to hear about *my* problems. Despite the cover illustration, though, there wasn't a single mention in the 30 pages of text of her seeking new quarters in a colonial mansion. Abandoned buildings, an animal pound, even a service station, but not once did she ever approach some Kentucky colonel to explain she was being kicked out of Farmer West's coop because Farmer West had died, and a new highway was going to be run through his place. That detail bothered me. It bothered me because the book's designer had apparently run amok, and Barbara had done nothing to head it off. If she didn't care about the misrepresentation, who the hell would?

Not Henrietta. She was as meek a hen as one could imagine. She hadn't wanted the task from the other hens to find new living arrangements before they all ended up on the butcher's block; she had simply been the only one of them without eggs to mother. But—after almost being cooked alive in the abandoned building, almost being caught by a cat in the pound, and almost being run over in the gas station—she had succeeded, finding new lodgings for everybody in a children's zoo. Even the rooster Henry, who had felt snubbed for not being given the house hunting job, congratulated Henrietta for her initiative. And Henrietta and Henry lived happily ever after in the children's zoo.

Henrietta was as much a hen, did hen things, as Squiggly did squirrel things and Wiggly Rabbit did rabbit things. All of Barbara's animals did exactly what their names said. They lived the most uncomplicated lives possible. They were simple to the point of oppressiveness—no secrets, no surprises, no scandals. Being plain didn't even cover it. They were arche-types at the same time they were ciphers. The one thing Henrietta didn't have were the lush colors Alicia's elves assumed as daily life. Barbara's plants, when there were any at all, were the grasses growing up between cracks in the sidewalk.

Even Johnny Iler seemed to have made progress before keeling over and being ditched in the wrong grave.

| 46 |

SILVIA BORGATO WAS big on streaming cigarette smoke—for the most part *near* your face, but if she happened to miscalculate, that was no tragedy for her, either. She was also just big—a good 170–180 pounds, 5'8", and long past being awkward about her out-sized gestures in tearing open sugar packets or crossing one heavy leg over another. When she didn't instantly catch my stumbling syllables, she squeezed her face into a scowl that could have short-circuited the coffee house's electricity. I thought I understood Borgato better by being extra careful when I spoke: Setting fire to a post office was the least I could do to work off my good behavior at home.

"Nullo was worthless. You know that, yes?"

"Mama!"

Nino had taken my arrival as an excuse to leave the waitering for the full house to Camilla and a teenaged boy and to flop down at our back table. At first, he had been entertained by my reactions to his mother's take-no-prisoners tartness. In the air was "*See, americano? How could I have turned out any differently with parents like these?*" But the more Silvia had insisted on how Nullo had brought her only grief, the edgier he had grown about his inclusion in such a package. "He doesn't want to hear this crap, Mama."

"He wants the truth. Don't you want the truth?"

"If it has anything to do with what I'm doing. I still don't know why you wanted to see me."

"Nino says you know all about this business. I want to know where the body is."

"I have no idea. Talk to the police or the hospital."

She threw Nino a withering glance: She had been down his dead ends before. "You said he could tell us something."

"He has connections. He can find out things."

"American connections, *scemo*! They've got the body they wanted, and they don't care about the rest of it. When did they ever care about anything in this country that didn't affect them directly?"

There is one advantage to being talked about in the third person: It gives you a chance to work annoyance up closer to self-righteous indignation. "Signora, if you want to talk to your son about me, fine. Just don't ask me to sit here listening to your bad manners."

Not even the glass Flavia had thrown at him in the nightclub had caught Nino so unawares. He looked at his mother in such alarm that the years peeled off him: He might have been an eight-year-old hearing the first cross thing ever said about his parents and not daring to think what the reaction would be. Silvia, on the other hand, wasn't so captivated. "I drove down here for information my son said you could give me. Do you know where Nullo's body is?"

"I have no idea."

"But you can tell us who we should be talking to, right?" Nino nudged.

"You could've done that yourself if you'd come out to the cemetery the other night."

That was news to the wrong person. "You didn't go out when they were digging up the grave!!??"

"The rain got my battery all wet. What, I was supposed to walk all the way out there?"

"He's your father! You could've shown more interest!"

And just like that she was out of energy—sitting back with a vacant stare, barely conscious of the cigarette between her thick fingers. She was as overweight mentally as she was physically.

"We're going to sue," Nino announced, seeing the floor was his. "And the lawyer needs a statement from you."

Hello, cow patty. "Saying what?"

"How the body was sent to America. How everybody over here tried to cover it up. The sister has to do the same thing."

"She's gone back to New York."

Silvia stirred enough for a contemptuous *sssss* and to drop an ash in the ashtray. He wasn't discouraged as easily. "Then you give the lawyer her address and she can fax him what she has to say. He says he needs both of you to swear about all this."

"About what exactly, Nino?"

"What do you mean about what? We spent money on a funeral that wasn't even for my father. We've had all this shock. Why? Because the hospital can't keep track of things. My lawyer says we have a big case. The worst that can happen, they'll make a settlement. If you're asking for something for your trouble . . ."

Where were Alberto Tortola and that second person who wasn't to be trifled with when you needed them? "Is this what you want, Signora?"

Silvia Borgato finally had a reason not to look at me through glass. "What I want, Signore, is to go back to Todi and not have to think about this anymore. I want to worry about the beans in my garden and the bastards who are trying to tear up the town center for one of their malls. I don't want to worry about Nullo anymore. I liked not worrying about him. But now these fools have made this carnival and I can't just ignore it. They always count on you to ignore things, Signore—in your country too, I'm sure."

Keep dissembling enough and you'll get around to everyone's role, even the Dottoressa Gallo's. "And suppose they admit it's their fault? That he got cremated by mistake and give you another document saying he's dead? That might be as much certainty as you'll ever have."

Nino didn't like her hesitation. "That won't be good enough," he barked. "We want more proof than that. And if they can't give it . . ."

"You'll want a million dollars."

"They do it in America all the time. Millions and millions."

"And what if your father isn't dead?"

This time her frown could have turned off the whole city's electricity, but he was too busy with the nightmare of millions flying out the window. "Yeah, right," he said. "They can't find him, so that makes him not dead. Let's see how far they get with that one in a courtroom. His own doctor will sign a statement saying she declared him dead. You didn't think about that, did you?"

No, I still hadn't, not in any responsible way. It had seemed enough to drop in the teaser for him, protect myself for the moment when he would see how doubly, triply vain all his money fantasies were.

He finally acknowledged the glares Camilla had been throwing him for not helping and trooped back over to the bar. His mother looked at me as though I had already spent their settlement. "It can take years to win lawsuits," I said, mainly to say something.

"You think he's alive, don't you?"

Minton: When up against a wall, and deservedly so, sweat. "No one has seen the body."

She had once worked for the Education Ministry? Well, she was marking my paper FAILURE. "If he is," she said, making an effort not to look behind me to Nino, "tell that *disgraziato* if I ever see him, I'll kill him . . . No, *zitta*! I don't care for me. I had enough of his art gallery whores and opera singers. If he lives or dies, it makes no difference to me. But for Nino . . ."

I remembered what Paola Restivo had said about people counting on deathbed reconciliations for wiping out whole lives of antagonism.

"They have never been perfect together," she said, reading my mind. "He liked the idea of a son, but not the boy. You think Nino didn't feel that? But he's still Nino's father and he owes him more than some farce . . ."

It went on like that for another minute or two. She had met him before he had developed his airs about being part of the cocktail party set. He might have been crude, but at least he had been honest and known his limitations. Where had all the pretensions come from? Not from her. And what had been her reward? Embarrassment and sluts who went to see the same American movies he did. What else could she have done but try to protect Nino from such garbage? That was why she had taken early retirement from the ministry and moved out of Rome when the boy had been a teenager. She had waited too long, had failed with Nino? Well, his father had failed before she had.

I couldn't, didn't want to, answer her. What I really wanted was for somebody in the coffee house to come over to the table and reassure me it was indeed wondrous that within the space of 24 hours I had gone from conversations where the assumption was that Nullo Borgato was dead to ones where it was a given, he was alive. Such a miraculous religious experience shouldn't have felt merely like a guilty conscience.

| 47 |

NINO FOLLOWED ME outside with his hangdog look. "She gets like that," he shrugged. "You didn't help her with the revolution 30 years ago, you're a fascist. Don't take it personally."

"You're going nowhere with this lawyer."

"It's what she wanted to hear."

"*She* wanted to hear?"

"That I'm doing something. If I do nothing, she thinks I don't care."

"Do you?"

He looked around uncomfortably. "That's my business. You'll help as much as you can, right? I'm not asking for guarantees. But if you can do anything at all . . ."

"What are we talking about, Nino?"

For the longest moment, his face was pure stupor—a five-year-old, a 10-year-old, even a 20-year-old, waiting to recognize something paternal in the Sunday evening traffic around him. But there was just honking and beeping and laughing and pedestrians running off to separate appointments. Not one of those passing gave us a second look. "Flavia. What else? She's got a lot of talent. More than that shrieking opera singer ever had."

And then he tossed away his cigarette and hurried back inside to help Camilla with the tables.

| 48 |

IT WAS, OF course, time to get drunk, preferably with people who had never heard of the Borgatos, Ilers, or Borlas. But who did that leave in my vast universe? It wasn't just the people I had interviewed over the last week, there were also those who had read an Italian paper or watched an Italian newscast over the weekend: They were all excluded, too. And scratch New York City and any place where an AP dispatch had relayed my story for Minton. In short, erase most of Italy and the United States. And what had Felicia Canton been doing since the Foreign Press Club bar? Informing Spain and Latin America about Lamberto Borla? So there went another country and another hemisphere. It *was* a small world.

So, unable to find the kind of company I could blame for it the next morning, I didn't get drunk. Instead, I meandered around the city on another spooling trek, waiting for every square, fountain, and basilica to reveal what I should do, at the very least shrug to me Nino-style that it wasn't important what I did. The most popular answer was gargoyles. Was it significant they all looked constipated? That most of them had lost parts of a limb or were spouting yellowish water into basins of cigarette butts and gum wrappers? I thought so. But beyond realizing I preferred their company to that of trolls or house-hunting hens, I didn't know *why* they were significant.

After a couple of hours of this, I was set to go back to the hotel for a sandwich and a beer. Then I saw a handful of people come straggling out of a side street movie house. The place had no marquee, just a couple of weathered posters stuck around a single glass door that needed a washing. The posters had earned their faded colors: They were for an ancient Clark Gable movie I remembered from TV as *Across the Wide Missouri*. Why not? I had crossed (and recrossed) the Tiber. Why not the Missouri, too?

Inside was a small, square box of a space that had the odor of a recently evacuated junk shop. Eight or nine rows of hard chairs requisitioned from some cell block had been screwed into the floor before a spotted screen that might have appealed to collectors of abstract art. There were only two other people in the place for what was going to be the last show—an Italian soldier who greeted my arrival through a leaden red curtain with an extended braying yawn and an old woman in a shawl who had fallen asleep. If the posters outside had made me think revival house, the inside said the only revival that went on in the musty air was of the occasional spectator. More likely, the theater owners had come across a print of *Across the Wide Missouri* in the rubble of some building collapse and had decided to cash in on their find.

Then the lights went from bleary to black and the MGM lion came on the screen; its roar was the last English I heard for two hours. I had known going in that Italy dubbed all its foreign movies, but what I hadn't known was that Italy didn't *completely* dub all its foreign movies. In striving for greater authenticity, the makers of *Across the Wide Missouri* had decided the Sioux characters should speak that language. Apparently lacking an Italian-Lakota dictionary, the Italians had kept those parts of the original soundtrack, so that half the picture was in Italian and the other half in Sioux.

At first, I just laughed, and got some glowers from the soldier for my trouble. He thought I was mocking him for not understanding what was going on.

"*Ma che cazzo! Cosa stanno diciendo?*"

"*Parlano indiano.*"

"*Indiano! Ma che cazzo! Sono io un indiano?*"

No, none of us were Indians. Who could argue with him? But big deal. Everything was so out of whack it was hard to remember when it had been *in* whack. Clark Gable opening his mouth and sounding like

Roberto Benigni being smothered. Adolphe Menjou twittering with a
Canuck accent, except that was only what I recalled from TV; the guy
doing Menjou in Italian sounded like Charles Aznavour on uppers.
Ricardo Montalban—Mr. Fantasy Island, Corinthian leather bullshit,
the wrathful Khan—doing it all in Lakota? And next to him, J. Car-
roll Naish, "Life with Luigi," answering him right back without a single
"how" or "forked tongue" in his Sioux spiel. Where had all this stuff been
when I had been studying comparative cultures at NYU? The soldier
was aggravated only about not being an Indian? There were all kinds of
things he could realize he wasn't if he would calm down and pay more
attention to the screen.

I made the list for him. He wasn't a son because his parents were
dead. He wasn't a husband because that required a wife. He wasn't a
reporter because reporters wrote stories, didn't suppress them. And that
was without counting the simpler things—the person who listened to
others sincerely, who volunteered for their confidences, who had loftier
goals than his own procrastinations. At least with Montalban and Naish
you knew how their debates were going by their gestures and facial
expressions—or, if all else failed, by the following scene of a powwow or a
massacre. Wake up, soldier, I wanted to yell at him. You want confusion,
watch *my* next scene, and tell me how the debate went.

It was a wonderful couple of hours. I slogged across the Missouri and
all the rivers east of it to where I was sitting. Along the way I lost some
people (Oscar the waiter and Annie), urged some others (Heckle and
Jeckle, Charles King, the Dottoressa Gallo) to walk into quicksand, got
separated from still others and wondered if I would ever see them again
(Barbara), but it was all standard trek fare. If there had been another
show, I might have stayed for that one, too—to be doubly sure Gable
didn't lose his scalp. But then the lights came up to their original glau-
coma level, and the soldier scraped out, slapping up every lowered aisle
seat to the back in irritation. And the old lady in the shawl, who had
apparently come awake with one of the deep chest coughs she had been
giving off during the picture, sat staring at the dead screen waiting for its
old stains to recompose themselves into my next move.

| 49 |

Paola Restivo wanted me to know I wasn't the one doing the favors. True, there was a taxi strike, and I would need two buses to get to her apartment, but that was what I was going to have to do if I really wanted her to take me to Borgato.

So I took the two buses, getting even with her by using the ride to dope out again why she was putting so much on the line. She couldn't have been the worst doctor in Rome if she was able to talk about having patients for 20 years. She might not have been a fashion magazine's flavor of the month for age or beauty, but she had her freaky charms and what our Style Page editor Romina Federoff had once described at The Ink as "an intelligent body." And maybe most important, she hadn't struck me as someone who gambled—even on lotteries, let alone on careers or romances. How did any of that add up to Nullo Borgato?

The kiosk where we were supposed to meet was at the bus stop. I had just enough time to collect a few morning papers when she drove up in a tan Mercedes. She didn't honk or look out the sidewalk window to identify herself; it was for me to get into or not what was being made available.

"You'll have plenty of time to look at them," she said, nodding at the newspapers. "We have a drive of about two hours."

"And you'd like me to keep quiet along the way?"

No, she wasn't in the mood for banter. She jerked back out into the traffic like a bad sport conceding a loss. The way she was dressed—scuffed boots, jeans, a thick green sweater under a gray jacket, white scarf around her head—told me we were heading into the country.

"You can go into a pharmacy dressed like this, too," she said, catching my look. "Why not rest all your guessing, read your papers, and I'll tell you when we've arrived, okay?"

I tried—at least until we were clear of the city and were clearly heading south, in the general direction of Naples. Only then did I stop fantasizing Gozzi had been keeping me under surveillance and would be stopping us with a roadblock at any corner. The happy note about the first part of the drive was that none of my four papers contained a new word about Borgato or Iler. Granted soccer was a national passion and sports sections around the world were twice as big on Mondays as other days, but to the point of reducing metro news to little more than a couple of pages of robberies and political speeches? What did that tell you about the place of professional sports in contemporary society?

"What is it you're afraid of finding?" she asked, after I had heaved the last of the papers into the back.

"Stuff I already know."

"That you know? You mean that you *don't* know."

"No, the stuff I know, I don't want other people telling me about it. They're wasting my time."

I didn't blame her for her look of beam-him-up-Scotty-before-it's-too-late. Of course, I should have been anxious about coming across something I didn't know; no reporter wanted to be scooped. Getting right down to it, I should have been grateful to all the Romas, Lazios, and Inters for kicking around the ball to the exclusion of everything else in the papers. But, it dawned on me, it was *only* as a reporter that I dreaded coming across some particular about Nullo Borgato I hadn't acquired first, that if I left Minton and my job out of the equation, I *did* want somebody from an Italian, Spanish, or Maori daily to tell me something I didn't know.

We came to a red light in the middle of EUR—Mussolini's wet dream of gigantic Roman statuary. She saw something funny on my face. "You think you're the only one tired of being told the same thing all the time?" she asked. "Who, as Piero would say, is always finding out Columbus discovered America?"

"That's your myth. We have Vikings, St. Brendan, even the Ainu. And that's without counting the Indians."

"So not only are we being told the same thing all the time, what we're being told is wrong!"

"Exactly."

She thought about it by tapping her index fingernail on the steering wheel; I had never thought of doctors wearing raspberry polish. "And when we refuse to hear it anymore—what is it we should do? Just close our ears? Resign ourselves that is human fate? Something like that?"

"Why don't you tell me how you decided to do all this?"

She needed the change of the light, but no more than that. "I've never been outrageous," she said, gunning the gas. "I never thought of that as good or bad, just how it was. Back in the Seventies, when this place sometimes felt like an armed camp, you could find me at a demonstration or at home studying. I could always make room for both, and felt I had to make room for both. These *qualunquisti* doctors who tell you they were more concerned helping individuals than Society with a capital S, they were hypocrites then and they are hypocrites now. Look at their medical careers, and you'll see most of them haven't been all that distinguished saving individuals, either. On the other hand, I didn't feel like just being another anonymous target for teargas, either. I was trying to learn a skill I thought was important and I didn't think I'd learn it any quicker having my brains smashed in by a police baton. So I suppose after a while I mainly showed the flag in the streets. If I knew the fascist gangs were waiting for trouble or the police were about to make a scene to help *Onorevole* Andreotti shuffle his cabinet, I usually stayed home."

"Did it work?"

"More or less. I opened my first little studio near the Chiesa Nuova with one of my instructors from Bologna. My first education was that this country is filled with hypochondriacs, people who are sure every twinge means it's time to call a priest."

I wondered if Johnny Iler had known that coming to Italy.

"My second education was I couldn't let that fact make me skeptical about real illness. Aldo, the doctor I shared the studio with, he used to say, 'Ah, yes, Paola, so much hypochondria, but they're still dying here as much as everywhere else in the world, so *some*thing fatal must be going around.' Result? I couldn't take hypochondria on its own terms anymore. Yes, the patient was a neurotic and needed attention or a psychiatrist or a new mother or whatever, but . . ."

"Even that might just be a symptom."

"Exactly! A symptom of something very physical. He's so concerned thinking his heart is about to stop beating because he doesn't want to talk about those terrible headaches he's been getting. The physical masquerades behind the mental by pretending to be physical."

"I thought you saw everybody as graph lines."

"I meant that, too," she said, sighing before a hilltop view of miles of small holdings to one side of the autostrada and endless marshland to the other. "It was all right *I* was never outrageous. I've made my peace with it, built a career with it. My parents lived into their seventies, didn't suffer much at the end. I thought about marrying once, then just felt that commitment start melting everything away. We parted friends. I bought an apartment. There was this one and there was that one. Nobody serious, but all of them serious. Did I want children? No, I didn't think so. And because I couldn't come up with a stronger answer than that, I figured the answer was definitely no. My own hypochondria? A scare three years ago, but here I still am. I miss smoking, I miss those extra cups of coffee. Would I like to look in a mirror again without feeling I have to come to grips with an adversary? Of course. And then there are these ex-communists apologizing for what they were, these fascists reborn as media moguls, and all these corrupt *mafiosi* of one kind or another pretending the 20th century never happened, maybe we should try a few of those things all over again and see if anybody notices. And this is without mentioning the situation in the Middle East." She finally looked over at me. "Do you understand?"

I understood nothing, especially why she had gone so abruptly from my reluctant chauffeur to an eager autobiographer. *I* would have never volunteered so much information about myself to me. I didn't like the association: The Talking Killer in the last scene who had nothing to lose explaining his crime because he was about to blow away his listener. "I'm sorry. I don't think I do."

She could deal with obtuseness, too. "It's one thing accepting *I'm* not outrageous," she said. "But why does all the rest of it have to be?"

| 50 |

SHE HAD MET Borgato at one of the Alberto Tortola soirees Alicia had mentioned. "A friend of mine, Ivana, knew him. She said he held his parties at home instead of at the store because he was afraid somebody would break something. But the house was like an antique store, too. Enormous glass cases with silver daggers and gold trays. Persian rugs on the walls. Jewel boxes on the tables. The time I went it was raining, and we put our umbrellas into this thing at the door Tortola said had once been in the Turkish parliament. A place for walking sticks?"

"I'll take your word for it."

She turned off the autostrada into a hilly side road. "Nullo came up to us and kissed our hands," she laughed. "Well, not kissed. Gave this soft blow he said was the right way to do it. He said it so clownishly I thought he was joking. But he wasn't. He'd discovered this fact about kissing hands somewhere and he wanted to show it off. It was like Ivana and I were teachers, and he was a student looking for a good grade. Then he asked how I liked one of Tortola's rugs. I said it was nice enough. He said it was from Isfahan. I said that was nice, too. And he said the one next to it, that was from Turkey and was the twin of one he'd had stolen from him by this American opera singer."

"Vivian Gertz!"

"Vivian Gertz. Came out with it just like that, less than two minutes after meeting him. Before I could stop him, he was telling me this atrocious story about breaking up with this singer—all the time with this beatific grin. Like he was a modern Job and that's what he had deserved, but wasn't it funny how it had actually happened? 'The funny thing about Vivian,' he kept saying, but there wasn't anything remotely funny about this Vivian or what she had done. To Nullo, though, it was all some kind of theater he had been privileged to be part of. I was fascinated. The stories, how he told them—blasé, but with hurt and chagrin right there—well, it was outrageous!"

She wanted me to smile with her, so I did. But she was still trying to persuade me of her ease in the Borgato mess more than I wanted to be persuaded. "They're bound to find out, Paola. Falsifying records. Fraud. The Borgatos alone. Nino's a loose cannon. You don't know what he's going to do from one hour to the next."

"And Silvia?"

"Her, too. She says she doesn't give a damn as long as Nino is okay. But she can wake up one morning and decide . . ."

Another nod. "Yes, Nullo says she can be very strong-willed."

"I'm not getting through here, am I? There're going to be consequences to all this. Today, tomorrow, next week."

She might have been annoyed at me or at the creviced road that was beginning to attack her springs. "No question about that," she said. "One of the consequences is pretty obvious."

"What?"

"How it's too late to go back now."

| 51 |

A GRAVEL ROAD off a road off a road finally brought us to a rickety white building; a rusting sign over the entrance announced it as an *osteria*. There were three dusty cars and a pickup truck parked under a pergola. Chickens were raising hell from somewhere in the back.

"It's lunch hour," Paola said, killing the engine and getting rid of her scarf. "Not much variety, but what there is is good."

She rocked heavily off her boot heels as she led the way inside, jingling her car keys with a reasserted proprietary air. The inside looked more like a butcher's than a restaurant. There was white marble everywhere—on the walls, the floor, the cash register counter, and what wasn't marble was still white. The only table occupied in the railroad car room was for four card players in the back.

"No more food in Rome?" A small man with a gray mustache didn't bother looking up from where he was siphoning white wine into a demi-john behind the counter. "Have to come all the way down to see Mario to have a good meal? Who's your friend?"

"Danny, Mario. Mario, Danny."

"*Americano?*" he asked, making the score about 96-1. The only one who hadn't tagged me instantly as, say, a Tunisian had been the old guard at the hospital my first day, and even he had thought being English was the same thing.

"*Stella!*"

It was only as he was rising from the card game and coming toward us that I realized my only physical preconception about Nullo Borgato had been Alicia's description—the balding man with the wide face and gold tooth. And she *hadn't* made him up totally, at least as far as the hairline and face were concerned. For all his stockiness, he moved lightly, almost airily. His smile (no gold visible) could have been an eagerness to please, a contentment he was pleased, or something in between. He wrapped his big hands around Paola's thin arms so confidently that, even though she was almost as tall as he was, she seemed half his size. "Nullo, this is Danny. He came all the way from America to meet you."

"The one who's going to cause all the trouble for me," he said, the smile still there but more vigilantly. "But not before we have lunch."

And with that, he darted off behind the counter, grabbed some glasses and an unlabeled green bottle from next to Mario, and darted back. How could you be furtive about staying in the open? However he managed it; his return made me feel as though I had wasted some last chance to escape. "Here's something I bet you never had in New York," he said, his voice a deep croon. "This is straight from the press. No sulfur or chemicals, just the grape. *Benvenuto*."

He was almost right. Only once before had I tasted the sweet-but-not-too-sweet mealiness of untreated white wine: a Christmas eons ago when my Uncle Joseph and Aunt Allie had brought three bottles to dinner and had insisted my father let the eight-year-old have his own glass of it. Bartering had been involved that time, too.

"And the good part is you can drink it all night and not wake up with a headache. Right, *stella*?"

"Which accounts for one part of the body."

"Always the doctor. You married, Danny?"

"A little while longer."

He laughed, she smiled curiously. "I know the feeling. You meet Silvia?"

"Yesterday."

"And Nino?"

"Him, too."

"The coffee house can do okay if he pays attention, don't you think?"

That sounded like three questions in one, and I didn't feel like answering any of them. "Why don't we order lunch?" Paola put in. "I haven't eaten today."

He didn't have to be asked twice to go scampering down past the card players to the end of the room and around a corner, apparently to the kitchen. "Of course, he's nervous," she said, settling her jacket around the back of a chair and sitting. "He has a right to be. And you—you and your wife are really divorcing?"

"Yes."

"You're relieved?"

I had never come right out and admitted that to anyone before, not even to Minton the night at The Ink when I had gotten high, but once I did, I felt doubly relieved. "That's the way it should be," she said, another return by her in-and-out no-nonsense chord. "You do something and, however long it has taken you to do it, there is this appropriate feeling."

"I'm not sure I understand *appropriate*."

"What is beyond you to have arranged personally, but what is still correct," she said. "We need another fork."

Borgato came back rhapsodizing about the penne and the rabbit he had seen in the kitchen and about Angelina, the cook Mario had been smart enough to marry. When the food came out after him, he turned his enthusiasm on the surrounding country that accounted for the best wine between Tuscany and Sicily, the oranges that were the envy of southern Europe, the mortadella that redefined cold cuts, and the artichokes that could be a meal in themselves if prepared properly. The rush was so effusive I felt myself edging away from the table, as if to get out of the path of some avalanche that would bury me under food and drink as the only natural concern for any human being worthy of being included within the species.

Then, finally, the question: "So what is it you want to ask me?"

From the corner of my eye, I saw the bearded man at the back table deliberately hold his card aloft, as though he too wanted an answer before taking another trick. "Ask? You're sitting here in front of me. What else is there to ask?"

He thought that was funny, and the bearded man flung down his card with a raucous victory cry. "How to say it? One little thing leads to another."

"Little?"

"Well, maybe one big thing," he conceded, not for a second breaking off his eating. "The morning the *professoressa* here came in and told me I might not last the day. You tell him that, Paola?"

"I don't like thinking about it."

"But it's true," he said, still finding something cheerful about it. "She said I had all this congestion, and it was worsening my blood pressure and on and on until there goes Borgato. I ended up in that bed for nine days. You know how I measured the time? Nino called me the first day, Silvia called me the fourth. And the Dottoressa here, of course."

"I had to be there."

"What she means is she came in three times a day. And except one time—just one time, Danny—she had to come with her stethoscope and all her professional questions. Don't you think a woman of her intelligence could have made a friendly visit to talk about something normal?"

"Like your crazy plan?"

"You still think it's so crazy?"

"Danny thinks it can't be done; someone will find out."

Their cool blew through every cavity in my mouth. "There's no *will* involved! Driving down here, I thought it was just you and Milano who knew. Now I see all these people . . ."

I shut up before the glare of the small, fat man who had been suffering through all the beard's tricks. Borgato didn't have to look behind him to see what had silenced me. "These are country people, and they are friends. You ask them what the weather is, they have to know you before they tell you."

"And Milano? Some night he drinks a little bit too much . . ."

"Piero is my cousin and a friend," she said tightly.

Borgato couldn't have agreed more. "People like Milano and Giorgio Principalli, they're good people."

"This Principalli knows, too?"

"He's a friend. Like Piero."

Count the ways Milano had blindsided me—not just about himself, but even about the money lender who had supposedly been such a threat at the funeral. "Next you'll tell me Tortola knows, too."

He thought his grimace was enough of an answer, but she didn't. "It's not a question of how many people know," she said, "it's who they are."

If I'd had a Bartlett's handy, I could have showed her a hundred and one quotations from statesmen, generals, and con men down through the ages refuting her. But I didn't have a Bartlett's; what I had were penne getting cold from my talking and a bizarre satisfaction for having been included in some exclusive circle that was actually about as exclusive as the population of Italy.

| 52 |

REPORTER OR NOT, I was definitely a tourist, and Borgato was bent on showing me all the sights. After we had gone through a warren of Angelina's rabbits and chickens, I followed him out to his dusty black Volvo for a two-mile trek to what he called his "land." While we waited for Paola to back out of the pergola and blaze the trail, I wondered where the money for any land had come from. From the doctor? From the obviously not so infamous Princigalli? Or were pensions for postal workers so good in Italy they could cover bribes for Danish prison officials and still be sizable enough to pay for property?

"*Cambiali*," Borgato smiled, as we crept down another bumpy road after Paola's car. "Just keep the paper going around. You don't do that in America?"

"That's why they invented credit cards. But I thought that was one of the cycles a dead Nullo Borgato was supposed to have ended?"

"What, I've crossed into Utopia, no more practical things to worry about? *Sei pazzo?*"

That was definitely a possibility, of course: Hadn't I already warned Minton I was another reporter from *Shock Corridor*, going mad on the beat? "You keep talking about everything like you've just decided to give up smoking or drinking!"

"It's exactly like that." he said blithely. "That life back there almost killed me. People who smoke or drink or eat too much, they get near death like I did, and they give up whatever's been making them sick. With me it wasn't cigarettes or wine, it was visibility."

"Visibility?"

"You understand? Always being seen by others?"

"I understand the word. I just never thought of it as a disease."

"Well, that's what it is," he said firmly. "And maybe when everything calms down in a few years, we'll be able to tell people."

"Tell them what? You haven't been dead all this time?"

"You don't think that day can come?"

"You're telling me you can see yourself someday picking up a phone and calling . . . !"

"Nino? Why not? Maybe by then he'll have made a success of something. I'm not saying it has to be the coffee house. One of these days somebody could walk in there with the kind of connections that will get him something better. That's one of the advantages of having a public business. You never know who's going to walk in the door."

It clearly being too late to worry about being buried under the landslide, I tried to concentrate on some of the individual rocks pinning me down. "And how do you think Nino or your ex-wife or anybody else will react when they see you walking up to them after so many years?"

He shrugged. "I hope they'll be happy to see me."

"Like you've just been in London or something."

"Of course, it will be a bigger shock to them than that. But there are always ways of leading into things so they don't get *too* shocked."

One way occurred to me immediately: Put Piero Milano on the job. He was twisty enough to smooth the path toward the Rapture.

"You don't think so?"

"What can I tell you, Nullo? You're way ahead of me. I'm still trying to figure out why you would go through all this trouble to hide yourself and then show up on somebody's doorstep."

"See?" he laughed, slapping me on the knee. "The idea's not so crazy after all. Even you believe we can get away with it until we decide to end it ourselves. I told Paola I could convince you!"

"You haven't convinced me of anything!"

"Because you haven't had time to think it out. How Nino would react the first time when he saw me again. Everybody dies, Danny. But then everybody comes back to life again."

"You don't say. And then what?"

He shrugged. "Same old shit starts over again, I suppose."

| 53 |

THE PROPERTY WAS a sloped acre of vines, orange trees, and lemon trees encompassing a squat brick house and shed. When we drove up, several men and women were working on the vines. "Harvest time. These are neighbors from down the road. When we finish here, I'll go help them."

Since the ultimate answer seemed to be infinity, I didn't bother adding the grape pickers to the column of How Many People Know Nullo Borgato Is Alive? In the house, Paola, who had begged off Mario's coffee at the *osteria*, was standing in her jacket in the narrow kitchen feeding the espresso machine. "Mario makes it much too strong. I think he must have Turkish blood."

"They're *contadini, stella*," Borgato said, embracing her from behind and kissing the nape of her neck. "When they get out of bed in the morning, they have to pull the sun out with them."

There was an answer, another crack, another answer. Had Minton ever said anything appropriate for the occasion? I couldn't think of a damn thing.

Finally, Borgato broke off his necking with an inspiration about what just had to go with the coffee and went sprinting out the front door. "I'm very happy with him," she said, as soon as he was out of sight.

"I know."

"I want to be sure you do. I don't want it ruined."

How often do we use the word *then* without thinking? For once, though, trying to return her severe look, I did think. So instead of coming out with a *then* that would have sounded like "okay, but you have to give me something back," I said: "There's something I'm missing here, Paola. And all that stuff in the car about being outrageous doesn't cover it. You're still risking too much. There had to be other, simpler ways."

Her only answer was to rub her palms down over her hip bones and turn to get some cups from a cabinet above the stove.

When Borgato came back, he had a bottle that looked like the first necessary step toward a Molotov Cocktail. It was grappa and having been made from the grapes on his land, was of course the greatest grappa anyone had fermented since the twilight of the Roman Empire. He talked about that, then about the house that had indeed been in the Restivo family for three generations, then about how he was counting on making the place pay for itself not only with the vines, but with the oranges and lemons.

I didn't listen all that carefully. One, because comfortable as the house was, its low ceilings and gesso walls had claustrophobia somewhere in my future. Two, because Paola was moving around so effortlessly—throwing off her jacket, constantly working the arms of her sweater, breaking twigs for a fireplace fire for the evening—that my questions to her began to feel irrelevant to the point of inanity. And three, having decided these people should be left alone, safe from the evil forces of the Gozzis and the Mintons, I was entertaining a kaleidoscope of those who had dropped out of sight never to be seen again. Jimmy Hoffa, of course. Judge Crater. That small boy in New York, Eton Patz. And what about all those taxpayers in Dallas and Saratoga Springs the IRS computers had mistakenly listed as dead instead of retired? And those were merely the obvious cases, the ones that had been celebrated because of crime or colossal stupidity. The grappa and I agreed there was only one conclusion: There had to be *thousands* of Nullo Borgatos! They were walking the earth as reverse vampires, the dead who were in fact living. How was one more going to make a difference?

"You like opera?"

Paola answered for him. "You can't let them do all the work," she said, nodding outside. "It wouldn't be fair."

Borgato knew she was right, but he wasn't ready to return the CD in his hand back to the stack on the window, either. "I don't mean Vivian," he said with a teasing smile.

She snapped another twig so that it sounded like an odd bone he would have to do without. "Damn right you don't. We don't have anything for the cats and dogs that will come running to the door."

He was delighted by her reaction. "Paola doesn't think Vivian was all that talented. Which is only half-true. Her voice, everybody loved it. But there is more to it than that, yes? The heart. The ambition to do something with the voice. Maybe she never wanted it that much."

Paola finally looked satisfied with her pyre. "He means she never wanted it as much as he wanted it for her. You can't live other people's lives for them, Nullo. They begin to feel robbed of themselves."

"So they try to make up for it by stealing back a few odds and ends." It was the jovial Job again: all chagrin, all hilarity, all target who deserved to be a target. "She got tired of looking for the right impresario, said she wanted to go back to America to teach music to children. Me? I don't want to hear about that. I have this new Callas, so I keep looking for the right maestro for her. What I didn't know was that she had already bought a ticket to go back. Then I start noticing things missing from the apartment. These Turkish rugs I took from Tortola on consignment. The buyer I had in mind had family troubles of one kind or another, so he kept putting off visiting me and the rugs stayed in the house. But then one day I come home, and I can't find them. Vivian says she was beating them on the balcony, a big wind came, and blew them down into the street. By the time she got downstairs, she said, the rugs were gone!" Even Paola matched his snort of a laugh. "And then there were these bowls—Chinese or something. I talked this old communist millionaire into coming by to see them, so I brought them home from Tortola. I show up with the millionaire one afternoon and Vivian says there's been an accident, she was sweeping and broke the bowls into a thousand pieces, so she had to throw it all out. This from somebody who didn't know what a broom was! But now every day she's beating rugs or sweeping floors like a maid!"

"What did you do?"

"What do you mean, what did I do? I checked with the *portiere*. Yes, he said, he had seen the *signora* going off to the post office a lot lately with big packages. Was that going to get the rug and the bowls back for Tortola? I accused her, she denied it, I accused her some more. I was exhausted by the time she finally left."

"You really ought to help outside, Nullo."

He polished off his grappa with a nod and a wave to me to go with him. I didn't know why I had to go anywhere. Vivian Gertz, the fat lady, had just sung, hadn't she? What else was there to know?

| 54 |

I ENDED UP with the lemons. The harvest foreman, a tall, spectrally gaunt man who used his frowns and stern stares for a voice, decided the market could bear badly picked lemons, but no way was it going to survive carelessly plucked oranges or don't even think about it, grapes. It took me a few minutes to believe I would be capable of even that much. Atop a rickety ladder that would have been a godsend for people trapped on the third floor of an apartment fire in New York, I had a Johnny Iler Moment: Maybe I was fatally acrophobic?

I got over it, and after a while didn't even bother yelling at Borgato whenever he moved his shorter ladder with the help of a few bangs on mine. If I was going to fall, I was going to fall, and that was just too bad for all those out there waiting to squeeze a little citrus over their fish. What bothered me more was that the foreman Renato had ruled that, even on his own land, Borgato couldn't be trusted to handle more than lemons, either. Hadn't the peasant-in-chief been told about the boxer and the knee-breaker?

"You do things when you're young," Borgato shrugged, picking away. "They seem exciting, they turn out not to be so exciting, and you get a few bangs for the experience. What can I say?"

"But this gangster stuff . . ."

"Gangster! The one I worked for, Moroni, he had a tailor's shop and a little *bisca* in the back room. One roulette wheel, two dice tables. The people who came were other shopkeepers in the neighborhood. They won a little, lost a little. If they won a lot one time, they lost a lot the next time."

"Were you just trying to impress Nino, or did you really beat up people for this Moroni?"

"I should have never told him that, that what you mean?" I couldn't imagine such bedtime stories inspiring Nino to become the Italian Minister of Justice, but on the other hand, I couldn't imagine telling him about the virtues of the World Court would have pushed him that way, either. "It happened a couple of times. But they were people who were cheating the cheaters, so it never bothered me. They'd open their doors like you were garbage left outside. They'd argue, I'd argue. A punch here and there."

"Until you ran into a cop, Nino said."

He almost teetered off his runty ladder in dismay. "He wasn't a cop, just a *vigile urbano*! Stood down near Piazza Venezia for years waving traffic back and forth. He learned judo or something from a book. When I swung at him, he pinned my arm, then hit me in the chest with his elbow. That didn't hurt me, but when I was falling, I tried to stop myself and pulled a disc. That's why Renato won't let me go up on your ladder. He doesn't want to be responsible for me falling and hurting my back again."

At least he had the dignity to avert his eyes with that bullshit, I thought; on the other hand, of the six or seven lemons he let roll out of his arms to the basket on the ground between the ladders, only two of them went where they were supposed to go. We both followed the rollers until they stopped. "We should get a bigger basket," he said.

| 55 |

WITH THE PICKING and basketing done for the day, Borgato had set up a card game in front of the fire for himself and three of the neighbors. Renato had huffed something about the banker's hours of city people and stalked off to the shed to dot some i's and cross some t's on the day's work. Paola had withdrawn to the bedroom with magazines she had brought with her. I had thought I was being clever by sitting at the window with a glass of grappa, waiting for Borgato or one of the others to ask whether I had ever heard of the game Scopone so I could play the innocent. Their reward for losing to me, I had planned, would be to confess that my Uncle Joseph had brought more into the house on Christmas than untreated wine.

Naturally, nobody asked, so I had to pay more attention to cloud lines and darkening tree palisades in the distance than I had counted on. Somewhere under the wispy clouds and behind the scrawny trees, I couldn't help reminding myself, was the banal glare of a Monday afternoon in New York where nobody was going to be exultant over my conversion to the whole, the rural, and the organic. But as long as I didn't budge from the window except to throw another twig on the fire, that still seemed more like their loss than mine.

"You don't have a game like this in America?"

Instead of from Borgato or one of the two constantly grumbling men at the table, the question came from Concetta, a prematurely gray, pleasant woman married to Grumbler Number One, Dante. Whatever the local code of stiff politeness toward outsiders required, she had been taking it far less seriously than her husband and Grumbler Number Two, Giovanni, peppering me with asides whenever a round was over, and the cards were being gathered up for another shuffle. Her I didn't want to trick, I decided.

"In New York they play poker," Borgato said with something like a whinny. "Games like this are too sophisticated for them."

Giovanni and Dante obliged with grunts, but Concetta looked at me with a twinkle that said it was time for us to spring the plan we had been working on for months. "I want to talk to Paola a few minutes," she said, pushing her chair back from the table. "I think he should take my place."

The grunts immediately became groans. When I told them I knew the rules, I was tempted by Concetta's delighted squeal to add I had picked them up, sophisticated as they might have been, by eavesdropping from the window. But I couldn't do it. Even before taking Concetta's chair, I had surrendered my edge by confessing about Uncle Joseph.

With what result? First, Dante sighed to himself that the mysteries of the world would always be baffling to him and Giovanni fixed me with a piercing stare to warn that, since I was to be his partner, I damn well better prove what I was claiming. Second, Borgato had the excuse for a giddy rhapsody on the incredibly rich cultural veins to be tapped within every home, movie theater, and fire hydrant in New York. And third, I was reminded of how long ago Uncle Joseph had died.

I didn't embarrass myself completely over the first half-hour. I even made a couple of pickups that earned nods from Dante and some pause from Giovanni. But I wasn't exactly the Cincinnati Kid, either. In one hand I had so many *denaro* suit cards and aces I should have let Giovanni help me sweep the table, but I gave him nothing to hold on to and we ended up with only a few tricks. It was still anybody's game.

Then the front door opened, and Renato stepped inside, his head precariously close to the ceiling. When Borgato asked sardonically if he was satisfied the way he had left the shed, the grave foreman set his eyes to the question as though being asked to provide an inventory, then gave a short nod and clomped heavily across the room to the kitchen. Neither Dante nor Giovanni appreciated the flippancy; for them, it was obvious, Renato was much more than a harvest supervisor and should have been treated with the utmost respect at all times. But if he was aware of having crossed a line, Borgato didn't show it; he just shouted over his shoulder that Renato would find the grappa atop the refrigerator.

As the game went along, Uncle Joseph's warnings about those who led with picture cards and about entire suits that appeared to have fallen out of the deck came back with more clarity. I had no trouble remembering how he had once sat on our couch hovering over the coffee table, rubbing his index finger over his salt-and-pepper mustache as he had studied his cards. I couldn't recall his voice exactly, but Giovanni's grumblings were enough of a replacement. After we had taken the lead, he even went so far as to fill in a reshuffling by asking how the weather was in New York. The Weather Channel had never seemed so helpful to human affairs.

Because my back was to the kitchen, I didn't think too much about Renato out there. At one point, I heard him murmuring to Paola and Concetta about the work that remained to be done the next day. But then, down to what could have been the last hand for beating Borgato and Dante, I felt him behind me. If ever the word kibitzer seemed inappropriate, it was with this silent shade of grim authority. And judging from the way Borgato and the others were guarding against looking up from their cards to him, I figured I was better off not being able to see his expression.

The showdown was a choice between aces: the sword ace or the money ace in my hand. One of them could get us the win, the other only another hand and the risk of blowing the whole game in front of the finish line. But which was which? Which one did I toss first and which did I keep for the very end? With only these two cards left, I lost sight of Uncle Joseph, not to mention Giovanni across the table. Minton had once said something pertinent to the occasion, hadn't he? The only thing that came to mind was his crack at The Ink one night that Frolich's pet Leo Rodriguez "couldn't organize a two-car motorcade."

I went with the sword ace. Borgato and Dante moaned in tandem. And a few seconds later, Giovanni and I had everything.

The hands came down on my shoulders so firmly I had an instant flashback to the night my father had grabbed me for trying to get out of the bathroom after sneaking a Camel. "*Gioca bene quest'americano,*" Renato ruled.

I didn't want his hands to move. I wanted them to stay there until he had testified for all to hear that Scopone was the least of it, that I played *everything* well. But then he lifted his grip, said goodnight, and moved regally over to the door and out into the night.

| 56 |

FOR PEOPLE I had known only a few hours, Dante, Concetta, and Giovanni left an unwelcome void when they begged off Paola's offer of omelets and salads and drifted out after Renato. Borgato seemed to feel it as much as I did, and he began making projects out of everything—gathering more wood from the shed for the fireplace, setting the table for supper, showing me his video collection. Didn't I like *Blade Runner?* How could anybody not have liked *A Space Odyssey?* Here, watch this scene.

I let the fidgeting go on longer than I should have. Finally, I told him I had no intention of telling Brooklyn and Queens he was still alive. He ejected *A Space Odyssey* from the VCR, then just nodded.

"But I still think I'm the least of your problems."

I hadn't heard Paola behind me until she said, "We'll take them one at a time. Thank you, Danny."

I didn't know why Borgato suddenly looked like he wanted to cry. I found out only a half-hour later, in the middle of supper.

There's the hoary joke about the boy who bicycles up to the United States-Mexican border at the same hour every morning. The customs people know he doesn't have a job, are absolutely convinced he's smuggling something past them, but never find anything in his saddlebags or pockets. Finally, years later, one of the customs agents, now long retired, runs into the kid and asks what it was he was smuggling all that time. "Bicycles, of course!" the kid replies.

Borgato and Paola made their confession halfway through our omelets. I had gone back to his breeziness in the car about reappearing one day in the lives of Nino and Silvia as though his faked death had never happened. Were they really thinking of doing it? What were the statutes on things like that? How could they know that showing up again after two years, say, would leave them immune to the Gozzis, as opposed to, say, reemerging after four or five years?

She let out a dry laugh. "I don't think the wait will be that long."

"But how can you be sure?"

She sized me up with one of her Mister Spock looks. I didn't know if she expected me to withdraw the question, withdraw from the room, or withdraw from their lives altogether. Then, without taking her eyes off me, she reached out for Borgato's wrist. "My graph says so," she said evenly.

He kept his head down over his plate, seeming to wait for her to let him go. "Paola's sick," he said.

And there went the whole warehouse winging past me—Kleins, Treks, Schwinns, Fishers, Cannondales. Borgato had been the ailing one, so focus on his illness as fatal or not. Doctors treated the sick, didn't get sick themselves. And this particular doctor? Well, wasn't she just something of a spinster looking for one last chance at mindless adventure—accent on the mindless and the purely stupid? Wasn't she her own best illustration of what was truly outrageous?

"I didn't know," I blurted.

"Of course you didn't. It's none of your business. Besides, if you need the prospect of another corpse to make up your mind about what to do, well, that wouldn't have been very educational for you, would it?"

I had the feeling that if I didn't smile with her, she would have never let go of the hand Borgato had put on her lap. "Touché, Doctor."

She went back to her salad.

She had been diagnosed with a recurrence of the cancer that had first shown up three years ago; now it had spread out beyond any optimism for the chemotherapy she would nevertheless take on one more time within a few days. She had found out about the recurrence exactly one hour before Borgato had been admitted to the hospital with pneumonia.

"I was in a very self-pitying mood. I thought he was going to die and I envied him. There would be much less commotion than when my time came. But then I got angry. I looked at him in the hospital bed, the oxygen in his nose, and I thought about all the seconds he must have lived thinking about this and wanting that and hoping this other thing, and all of that would have been for nothing if he just slipped away. Of course, it was easier thinking about him instead of myself that way, but the difference really didn't seem to matter. It was exactly the same for both of us. So many things we seemed entitled to. But in the end, they came down to one thing only—we were entitled to *more than we had been*."

I had a sudden vision of Joe McAteer breaking through the door. "*Entitled? Nobody's entitled to anything! Bums should work, the starving should beg, and the dying should get on with it!*"

"I didn't say anything until Nullo was better. I had decided I was going to be the one who disappeared. I wanted to come down to the house here, be away from all my graphs. But then Nullo reminded me of the obvious—that would have just been the final tracing of my graph. Nobody would have raised an eyebrow if I did that. That's what everybody in my condition does. They withdraw and they wait. I would have been doing exactly what would have been predicted. Nullo said it had to be him. There would have been something unexpected about that. Something aggressive and arrogant and, yes, even exciting."

"What I really said," he corrected gingerly, "was that there were people who still need her. For however long she can go on, she has patients who depend on her."

"And I still say there are other doctors . . ."

"That's not the point, *stella*. There's no reason for you to abandon them. Me? The people depending on me were doing it for the wrong reasons. I wasn't indispensable to them. I had so little to lose compared to her. If one of us could start over for both of us, it had to be me."

"And you really think of down here as being new . . . ?"

He laughed. "You mean Renato and Dante? Yes, they'll always think of me as the incompetent city boy. They think I know as much about grapes as people in Rome thought I knew about American science-fiction movies. Fuck them all for that. The important thing is we are together."

"In a way we have created," she finished.

"But that's . . ."

"An illusion!" he whinnied until she was laughing at me, too. "Of course it is! But that's all right. It's ours, not the post office's, not the Party's, not Vivian Gertz's, not the illusions on television all the time!"

"And it has a time limit," she added evenly.

He could have done without that reminder.

And so could I have.

| 57 |

THEY WANTED ME to stay for the night and return to Rome with her early in the morning. But as soon as I heard about a 10:00 bus only a few miles away, I knew I had to get going. What was it I had been worrying about after meeting Barbara the first time—feeling like a fifth wheel? Hanging around the farmhouse, forcing the two of them to be evasive about wanting to be alone in the bedroom, would have been worse—feeling like a fifth wheel already out of air. He would drive me over to the bus, and that was that.

She lingered at the front door with me while he went ahead to see if the night cold had done anything to his whimsical battery. She looked so in command of that "intelligent body" of hers I couldn't believe morons were already tearing her apart inside.

"Maybe we'll see each other in Rome."

"I think I'm going back to New York tomorrow."

"I was talking about your next trip."

What could I say? I wouldn't have accumulated enough vacation time for months and by then she would be dead? "Very soon," I said.

"Good."

I started to kiss her, but she beat me to it. A kiss on the cheek, one last look at her raspberry nails as she rubbed her chin, then she was scooting inside and closing the door after her.

"You probably feel blackmailed." Borgato waited to say it until we had bumped away out of sight of the house. Since I didn't have a coherent position on the issue, I didn't answer him.

"What is it they say when they give those lifetime awards to people who are still alive? They always joke they are surprised and maybe they should lie down and die. I'm getting that kind of award, Danny, and the last thing I feel like doing is lying down and dying." He braked as something hopped across the road in the headlights; he had adapted enough to his new surroundings not to be caught by the odd hare or fox. "I spent a long time trying to feel useful. But it always felt more like *trying* to be than actually being. I stopped thinking about it. Doing what I was doing, being with the people I was, acting the clown who wanted others to put up with me—it was all the same. When I went to the hospital, I really wasn't all that frightened. The doctors in the emergency room made me nervous with all their running around, but inside I wasn't afraid for myself. Living and dying really didn't seem to be so different."

"But you had Paola."

"I know. But I wasn't any more honest with her than I had been with Silvia, Vivian, or anybody else. It was only when the crisis passed and then she told me about herself that I felt this fear about losing something I didn't want to. And . . ."

He shook his head; the big face saw more than hares and foxes on the other side of his wheel. "And? And what?"

He recognized what he saw. "And even that wouldn't kill me," he nodded. "I'd get used to it. We would be together while she was dying and I would feel useful again, like looking around for an impresario for Vivian. Nothing would ever come of it. She would die, just like Vivian would go back to America someday. But I could account for myself in the meantime by being . . . what?"

"Loyal? Faithful?"

He half-blurted, half-splashed a laugh. "Christ, no! The best part of looking for Vivian's impresario was meeting their secretaries and assistants. Would I have been more faithful to Paola? Nothing makes me think so."

"So how would you account for yourself?"

"By being there, just by being there."

"Is that a lot?"

"*Niente.* That's why as soon as she started talking about resigning from the hospital, I knew that wouldn't have been enough for either of us. Too many people would have known she was down here. And maybe once a month, on the weekends, they would drive down for a visit to see how much worse she was than last time. What kind of escape would that be? It wasn't her life she had to escape, anyway. She didn't have to try to be useful, she *was* useful. She saved lives, gave people hope. So okay, we'll do something radical. We'll make ourselves only for ourselves. The excitement of the race. The fun of hiding. Swearing this one to secrecy. Making decisions about our oldest friends—who can we tell, who can't we tell? An illusion, like you said, but I don't feel just *there* anymore. I've died, Danny. And I know she can depend on me."

He insisted on parking and getting out of the car with me while I waited a scheduled four or five minutes for the bus. The stop was little more than a pole on a hilly curve; three other people, all with bundles or packages and looking like regular commuters, were already waiting.

"You'll see Nino again before you leave?"

"I don't think so."

He nodded to a poster for Campari across the street; in profile, there was definitely something of the pug in his features. "Flavia still around?"

"Yeah."

"How good can she be if she's fooling around with him instead of getting some serious manager?"

"You talking about Flavia or Vivian?"

He gave me a mock frown. "Don't think I didn't think the same thing sometimes. I know Vivian did."

"But at least she got rugs and vases out of it."

"I've always wondered why Tortola didn't put up more of a fuss. I like thinking Vivian brought the stuff to somebody in New York and he said, 'Turkish rug! This is an old mat from a Turkish bath! And these Chinese vases—it says right here they were made in Turin!'"

"But you don't have to believe everything back there was a fraud, do you?"

"No. But that part of it, yes. Otherwise, I'd have to believe she robbed me of millions!"

Laurel and Hardy came back for the final couple of minutes. Sure, we would write to one another. But he couldn't write to me at the house because I wouldn't be living there much longer. And the paper? Even if I were still working there, it wouldn't be the smartest thing in the world to have a letter from Nullo Borgato going through mailroom hands. On the other hand, writing in care of Paola at the hospital didn't seem like a long-term plan, either. So maybe the best avenue was Mario at the *osteria*.

He finished scribbling down the address as the bus trundled around the bend. "It will all be okay," he said, handing me the piece of paper.

"Like Paola said, it's too late to go back now."

Five minutes later on the bus, I could rationalize leaving it at that. Of course, there were a hundred other things I wanted to know. And for his part, just for openers, he hadn't exactly put me through the third degree to find out what part of Puglia my grandfather had come from. How self-absorbed could the bastard be? But, as I told myself slouching down next to the window, those were details for the next time—in person, by letter, by e-mail if he ever installed a computer next to his VCR. Then and there, it seemed enough just to return his hug and think the good thought—that Paola would come up with more graph paper.

| 58 |

MAYBE IF I had gotten back to the hotel before two o'clock, with the bar still open and a guest or two still hanging around, I wouldn't have felt as though I were walking into the Alamo after all the bodies had been dragged off and I was just in time for taking on the second charge by myself. At the very least, I should have been satisfied asking the night porter for my key and leaving my messages in the box until the morning instead of holding out my hand for them.

Renato wouldn't have congratulated me for how I played the cards I spread out over my blanket. Obviousness was my only strength. Minton, for example, was definitely last for time reasons. And Alicia, who apparently hadn't heard John Iler was yesterday's news, was almost as clear—maybe a call from the airport just before I stepped on the plane. And Annie, she was going to be first no matter how sure I was that only an answering machine awaited me on the other side of the ocean.

Onto the bigger thorns. There was no way to brush off Cleary. He might have posed the biggest threat of all to Borgato and Paola, even more than Gozzi. Not only did he know about their relationship, he had informed me of it and expected a buck back for his quarter. The alternative was all those other employers he liked alluding to between shakes.

Felicia Canton? She was Cleary without the shakes, and she had an interest in Lamberto Borla nobody else had. "Needs to talk about living survivor idea" was the message the clerk had transcribed at one in the afternoon. Did she still have that need or had she squeezed enough out of Cleary at the Foreign Press Club bar to move on to Paola by herself?

Chet Winans? He should have been as obviously postponable as Minton and Alicia, but something told me not to be hasty. And Barbara? Had she just wanted to be sure I could still be in a dreamland called Rome? Had she gotten through 24 hours, decided she hadn't missed me, and wanted to say she preferred keeping it that way? Or had she just been anxious to hear what I thought of Henrietta's search for a new house?

Annie was home. "Daddy died this morning."

I was sorry for her, I was able to say I would be back the next evening, and I felt like vomiting out the thought that the last two women I had slept with were busy with funerals in New York. There had to be a god snickering somewhere that I had crossed the Atlantic to straighten out cemeteries while business had never been better in those I had left behind.

"We'll have the wake tomorrow and Wednesday, the Mass Thursday morning. You'll be back?"

"I just said I'll be back tomorrow."

"Seriously. If you can't make it, it's okay. I'd just like to know."

"Annie . . ."

"All those cousins from Maryland are going to be here. I just don't want to get into 20 Questions with them about where you are."

"Standing right next to you."

"Oh."

"Annie?"

"I know you didn't like him. Can you really make it back?"

When I hung up, I sat with the phone on my lap a long time. The dead Joe McAteer was harder to deal with than the living one. I had been able to depend on the living one for some lunacy that forced Annie to think about being a wife as much as a daughter. Now I had lost my ally. She didn't have to worry anymore about his outbursts, so she didn't have to be protective of me anymore, either. Of course she felt abandoned. So did I.

For all the paper around me, I had to admit, last place was second place. Minton didn't like his standing under either name. "I know they're busy getting ready for one of their World Cup games over there and need you to advise them," he said, "but I thought you went over there for something else."

"Most of what I know is in the story I sent."

"*Most* he says."

It was time to go on the record. "Borgato's dead. They just lost the body somewhere, and I don't think they'll ever find it."

There was no bolt of lightning, but he began sounding like he was breathing through his bottom teeth. "That's not what Rodriguez says."

"What the hell does Rodriguez know?"

"About where our money goes when we lose it in the stock market, not much. But he's always checking in with our Latino friends and he tells me *El Diario* is going tomorrow with something about this Borla guy. Something picked up from the Spanish agency."

"Felicia Canton," I said, hoping my command of that fact insinuated more.

"Exactly. And according to Rodriguez, she's putting it out that this actor guy Borla and Iler are the only stiffs in our saga, that our other friend is still alive."

"Bar talk, Ed."

"The same bar where you heard it?"

It was a fallback position; not a liar, simply an incompetent. "As a matter of fact. I checked into it. One of the doctors at the hospital, it turns out, knew Borgato personally . . ."

"Right. That's what the Latinos have."

"So she knew him. So what? You think even a lover is going to risk her career for something like Canton is suggesting? Borgato's no fugitive. The Mafia's not looking for him, the IRS isn't, the Mossad isn't. What would be the point of a big charade?"

There was a longer silence, and I thought it would have been nice to see what Canton had actually dumped into her piece. "That was my question, Danny Boy," he said finally. "And this piece in *espanol* doesn't help too much. We got this guy playing Hamlet and rebels getting guns and on to the next town where he played Brutus. And somewhere in the middle of all this is a plot to hide bodies. Confuses an old man."

"Me, too."

"But then I'm thinking. There are so many byways and highways in the human heart, you never know where the next speeder is going to come along. Take you. You need a break to get away from some domestic strife, so Easy Ed is accommodating."

"Meaning what?"

"People do crazy things just to get away from the personal."

"You're the one who sent me, Ed."

"Generally speaking, I mean."

"Borgato was divorced and liked the doctor. He had no reason to get away from her."

"You talked to her?"

"I said I did."

"No, you said you 'checked into it.' You actually talked to her and believed her?"

"Ed . . ."

"Okay, okay. That's your non-story."

"Yeah, I guess so."

"Okay. I'm sending Ward to cover the Iler burial tomorrow. Is there anything he should know?"

"Nothing I can think of. You want a wraparound?"

"No, our budget has room for only one story for every bacchanal in Europe. We'll talk about it tomorrow. You'll be in, right?"

Whoops; not even. He listened to me about Joe McAteer, sounding a lot more sympathetic toward me than I had toward Annie. "Maybe you can jump in for a few minutes Wednesday."

"Thanks, Ed."

"Danny?"

"Yeah?"

He cleared his throat. "Not many of us are where we should be when somebody dies. Not even the fucking global village is ever going to solve that one."

All I had to do was press my finger down on the receiver strip. But that suddenly seemed more cowardly than abandoning a regiment to slaughter. "What about the opposite, Ed? What about not being in the right place when somebody decides to live?"

He laughed. "Yeah. We'll include that spooling topic when we see each other at The Ink Wednesday. Have a good trip."

The click felt like permission to go to sleep.

| 59 |

CLEARY WASN'T SURE he wanted to say goodbye to me over coffees at his Piazza Navona hangout. If he was disappointed I didn't want to make more of his lead on Paola, he was also tantalized by the prospect of having the field to himself as soon as I got out of town. His compromise was to postpone things by inviting me to lunch. "So you'll have another meal on the plane. On a diet?"

"I'm not really up for it, Fred."

"Even first-class on Alitalia isn't what it used to be. Strictly Airline Italian. Back in the days when they were competing just against TWA and PanAm, they put more effort into it. Then Reagan starts the deregulation ball rolling . . ."

Walking over to the cafe, I had considered several tactics for keeping him away from the farmhouse. All that had gotten me was a dull feeling that elaborate lies and straightforward honesty would have been equally ineffective. Was there such a thing as a workable hybrid of the true and the false? Watching him use both his hands to bring his tea to his mouth, I knew I had to swim for it. "Paola Restivo is dying of cancer. The Borgato thing hasn't lengthened the outlook for her."

He looked genuinely perplexed. "You know this for a fact?"

"I spoke to her. You were right about the two of them—they did have a thing. But right now, she really doesn't need people like you and me pestering her with idiot questions about how Borgato might still be alive."

He nodded noncommittally. "My brother called yesterday from London. Says he's on a business trip and wants to hop over for a quick visit. The condition I'm in, the last thing I need is my family expecting me to guide them around the city."

"And you're not even dying."

His index finger and thumb needed a couple of tries before getting at the cigarette in his shirt pocket. "Tell that to my nervous system."

"You know what I mean, Fred."

Not the happiest of openings; he lighted his cigarette with a new dose of shrewd and canny. "What makes you believe her? She could be trying to divert you."

"Call me superstitious, but I'd come up with a better story than giving myself cancer."

"Iler seems to have done that all the time . . . Just a joke."

"I believe her. You don't, you can always make one of your famous phone calls. There's got to be a record of her illness in that hospital."

"That's right."

He said it so tartly I was supposed to take it as a warning, reminder, and challenge all in one. "What the fuck is that supposed to mean? We back with your X-Files conspiracies? Save them for Felicia Canton. You find out Restivo blindsided me, more power to you."

"Don't get your drawers in a knot."

"Then stop acting like we're sitting in the Casbah. John Iler is dead."

"But is Nullo Borgato? Isn't that the question?"

"Find him alive and Minton will walk your check over here personally and offer you my job."

Some people would say stringers on the sauce aren't exactly energizer bunnies to begin with. But with somebody like Cleary, I knew, there were usually periods of energy—days, maybe weeks, when he took vitamins to chase the hounds back to Hell if that was what he had to do. What it came down to was trying to stall his next burst of enthusiasm until Paola and Borgato were further along their road.

"You like playing with people, Danny?"

It was the bolt of lightning I hadn't heard lying to Minton. His gaze followed the tendril of smoke from his cigarette until it disappeared. "You probably haven't even got a guarantee from Minton on all those promises you've been making," he said. "That's no minor thing to me, you know. I have to have a woman in almost every day now because I can't clean my place myself. And it's not just the expense, either. You can't find these old-time immigrants from Calabria or Sicily. Now they're university graduates with tiny asses and they make you feel like you're the one wasting their brains because they have to use a dust rag . . ."

He was right, of course: I *couldn't* guarantee a goddamn thing, not to him about Minton and not to Borgato and Paola about him. If there was anyone still sitting around in his fez in the Casbah, it was me. "Want the truth, Fred?"

"That might be refreshing."

"When I saw Restivo . . ."

"I'm talking about Minton and that little IOU you gave me the other night," he said testily. "Screw all these dead and dying people. I'm still alive, fuck it, I'm good at what I do, and I expect to be compensated for it. Can you or can you not get some money out of the paper for the help I've given you?"

Believe in melodrama. Believe in people misunderstanding one another, walking in the wrong door at the wrong time, entering a phone booth seconds ahead of a kidnap victim and picking up the receiver to hear the abduction terms—all starring your favorite movie actors. Believe in melodrama and the imagination opens up—if necessary, for instance, concocting a tale so that I could give a few bucks to Accounting and Accounting could write a check to Fred Cleary. And who said that would even be necessary?

"I told you you'd get your money, and you will."

He looked disoriented. "Really?"

"Really."

"Okay, then."

"Just don't fuck me over, Fred. I promised Restivo we wouldn't bug her anymore. Don't make me a liar."

He shrugged. "I'm tired of this crap story, anyway. Remind Minton there's a lot more going on over here with the living. The Filipinos moving in. This cut-rate Rupert Murdoch trying to turn the country back to World War I. A new Hollywood on the Tiber . . ."

I looked over at the piazza's central fountain. The legend was that Bernini had his central deity raising his arm to fend off having to see the ugliness of Borromini's Basilica of Saint Agnes across the street. That was melodrama too, I told myself. And both the fountain and the church were still standing, right? So who cared about all the petty emotions that had gone into their survival? As Nullo Borgato understood, the trick was to outlast the pettiness.

| 60 |

I WENT BACK to the hotel to pack. I thought about calling Felicia Canton, then decided against it. Unlike Cleary, she seemed immune to melodrama, was probably more absorbed by the mathematical prejudice that three into two didn't go. Short of coming up with a new universal number theory, I couldn't see myself persuading her of anything. She would follow Lamberto Borla deep into the Amazon and eventually come out of the jungle knowing about Borgato and Paola or not knowing about them. I could only hope she would stay lost for a while.

I threw both Alicia's painting and Flavia's photos into my bag. What I would do with them I had no idea, but I knew that whatever it was, even tossing them into New York garbage, would have required more decision than leaving them behind in a hotel room.

I didn't have to call for a cab. Chet Winans, who seemed to have taken up residence in the lobby, phoned up to say he had accompanied me into the city, so it was only proper he escort me out of it. Whatever last mission he was on for King, I told myself, had to be cheaper than a taxi.

He waited until we were clear of the city to end his discourse on what the Phillies would need by spring training to announce his news. According to Gozzi, the Dottoressa Gallo was out and her scrupulous assistant Rinaldi was in. Even the most preliminary of inquiries had turned up other questionable burials before anybody had ever heard of John Iler.

"So maybe Barbara wasn't so far off," Winans laughed. "Everybody in the ground may be in the wrong place."

"And this was worth ruining your siesta for?"

"Well, I just thought you should have the context. We didn't screw up on Iler, they did."

"I already told you I didn't think that was your job."

"Yeah, well. It's always good to cross the t's. I'm not saying you, but American diplomats are always easy targets for certain media elements." He looked perfectly serious. "Tell me it's not true."

"Where do you learn to talk like that? 'Certain media elements?'"

"We're all just doing our jobs, Danny."

"No, we're not, Chet. We're talking about corpses. If that had been Borgato or Borla in the casket sent to Kennedy but the nameplate had said Iler, nobody would've been the wiser. This has all been about nameplates."

He was offended. "That's a helluva thing to say! People have been put out by this mess. They've suffered, not known what the hell . . ."

It came on me just as we were passing a billboard for a movie where everybody looked a little dopey trying to look smart. I hadn't had anything all day except for a caffe latte for breakfast and a second one with Cleary, but suddenly my stomach felt like a drop bag for unpleasant things. "Pull over a second."

"Here?"

"Just do it, will you?"

Being the bratty soldier he was, he waited another quarter of a mile before finding a shoulder away from the Indy 500 drivers behind us. By then I didn't care if I erupted in his front seat or not. But then the car was still, and I had to supply all the motion—opening the door, feeling the lead weights that had filtered down into my calves, barely getting over to the yellow and brown weeds before letting go. And even that was exasperating. There should have at least been that illusory moment or two when my chest and stomach winked at each other that everything was going to be all right now that they had dispelled the garbage; but no such thing. My throat was calling the tune, and it wasn't at all pleased with the way things were going. It was going to scratch and send out for hiccups; screw what the downstairs neighbors wanted to feel good about.

You go with the flow, even when it's an iceberg. I thought of all the things I wanted out of me, and I immediately had a Cecil B. DeMille cast. Except that none of them were people. Summoning up the likes of Tortola and King and Heckle and Jeckle did nothing. They had never wormed their way deeply enough into me to be spat out. Nino? Winans? No, I finally listened to my throat, it was the abstractions that counted most. It was the sliding and sidling and insinuating and implying and lying. It was the gooey clothes attiring decisiveness and clarity and judgment and opinion I had digested. It was the simplest thought as tar, the blandest remark as mustard, the smuggest silence as rancid mayonnaise. These my throat understood and, finally, held back the hiccoughs to let my chest try again. And this time even bile accepted it wasn't going to get too many more chances and dove out into the weeds.

I saw little of it. Because the field where I was standing was sloped over some kind of runnel, I could see only the most minute traces of splat on the dead vegetation. It took me a long moment of staying bent over to realize I didn't care that it was even appropriate the weeds in me be obscured by the more important weeds visible to thousands of drivers every day.

"There's been a flu going around," Winans said behind me. "Looks like you're taking it back as a souvenir."

A paunchy Jumbo with a scimitar as part of its logo looked near enough to scale as it dropped toward the airport, still miles away. I didn't know what the dots were, but when I finished connecting them, the plane reminded me to call Alicia Silvestri before leaving.

| 61 |

"HE DIDN'T HAVE a gold tooth."

"I know."

"I was confusing him with somebody else from Tortola's."

"I don't think so, Alicia."

"What?"

"Borgato doesn't have a gold tooth, and neither does anyone else."

"You sound like you have been drinking."

"I'm not saying there aren't people with gold teeth. Just not the ones in your head."

She shouldn't have paused; it forced me to smell my breath. "You are saying you know my private stories?"

"I admire them."

She giggled. "I don't think so."

"I do. I just didn't understand them until I figured out you *started* with your happy elves; you didn't escape to them."

"That's . . . right."

"What you escaped to were the Johnnys, and they made every second with the elves even better."

"I never worked as much as after Johnny moved in. Those walls in my living room were almost bare. I didn't believe enough in the happiness of the elves. They always came out looking so sour. Why would I want that up on a wall? They would have been like Barbara's animals—always working, working, looking for something even they know will never make them happy. It would have depressed me to live with that. "

"Tortola agrees."

"Forget him. He's a philistine. He doesn't know the difference between art and interior decoration. I take it as a compliment my work is in his back room."

"We were talking about Johnny."

"Yes, and I miss him. I don't expect you to believe that, but I do. I wasn't pretending when I became a little emotional with you about him the other day in the kitchen. He let me believe in my work. I couldn't say that to Barbara. She wouldn't have understood. Her whole life revolved around Johnny, and of course that's absurd. Nobody's life should have ever revolved around him."

"Your work is all that mattered?"

"You can depend on it. You can like it. You can love it. And you can be grateful sometimes to the people who let you feel that way. It is a way of staying in contact with the . . . .Johnnys."

"It's not enough, Alicia."

"For you, maybe not. You're younger than I am. Or maybe you're just doing the wrong work."

"I don't want a Johnny Iler as my fable."

"Of course you don't. You're too much like him in some ways. Johnny was curious about nothing. Are you curious about anything besides what they pay you to be curious about? I warned you about worrying too much about money. It blocks out more important things."

Even under the heading of sentimental goodbyes, she was pushing it. "Maybe you should go fuck yourself."

"Maybe," she laughed. "That has its moments, too."

"I'm sorry. I shouldn't have said that."

"Say what you want, *caro*. We owe each other nothing."

"Is that the ideal?"

She didn't have to pore over that, either. "For some of us. For me. For Johnny. For the sister too, I think. You, I don't know. Maybe you should get another job and see if you're still curious about things. Then you'll know if it's your ideal, too. Have a good flight, Danny."

| 62 |

I FLEW BACK to New York for a funeral with a pretty clear idea about who had died.

Joe McAteer, my favorite gargoyle, had died, too.

ABOUT THE AUTHOR

DONALD DEWEY has written some 40 books of fiction and nonfiction, as well as contributed scores of stories to magazines and other periodicals. He has also had some 30 plays staged in Europe and the United States. Donald's awards include those named after Nelson Algren and the Actors Studio. Dewey is a widower with one son and lives in Jamaica, New York. At one point he lived in Europe for 14 years, writing screenplays and working for the Italian news agency ANSA. Dewey was editor of the ASME-award winning magazine Attenzione and was editorial director of the East-West Network, overseeing a dozen in-flight magazines and the PBS organ Dial. He has also been a theater critic for WNYC in New York and spends far too much time for his health watching the Mets.